JGN STRATFORD
The Stratford Zoo
Midnight Revue present
Lendler, Ian,
33341005535033

STRATFORD ZOO

MIDNIGHT REVUE PRESENTS:

MACBETH

STRATFORD ZOO

MIDNIGHT REVUE PRESENTS:

MACBETH

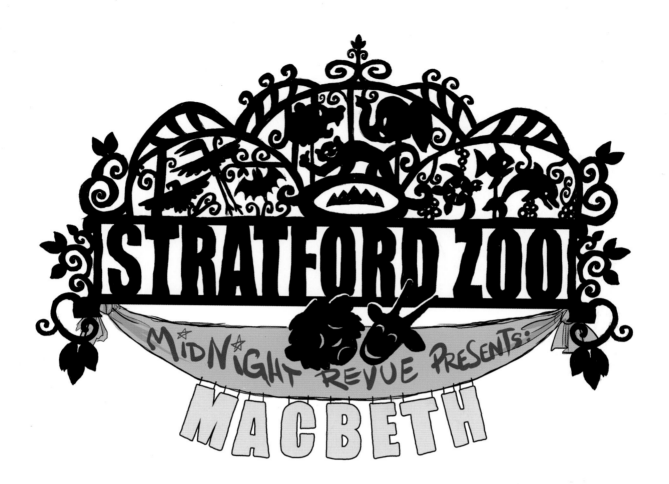

Written by Ian Lendler
Art by Zack Giallongo
Colors by Alisa Harris

:01
First Second
New York

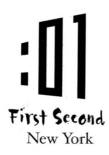

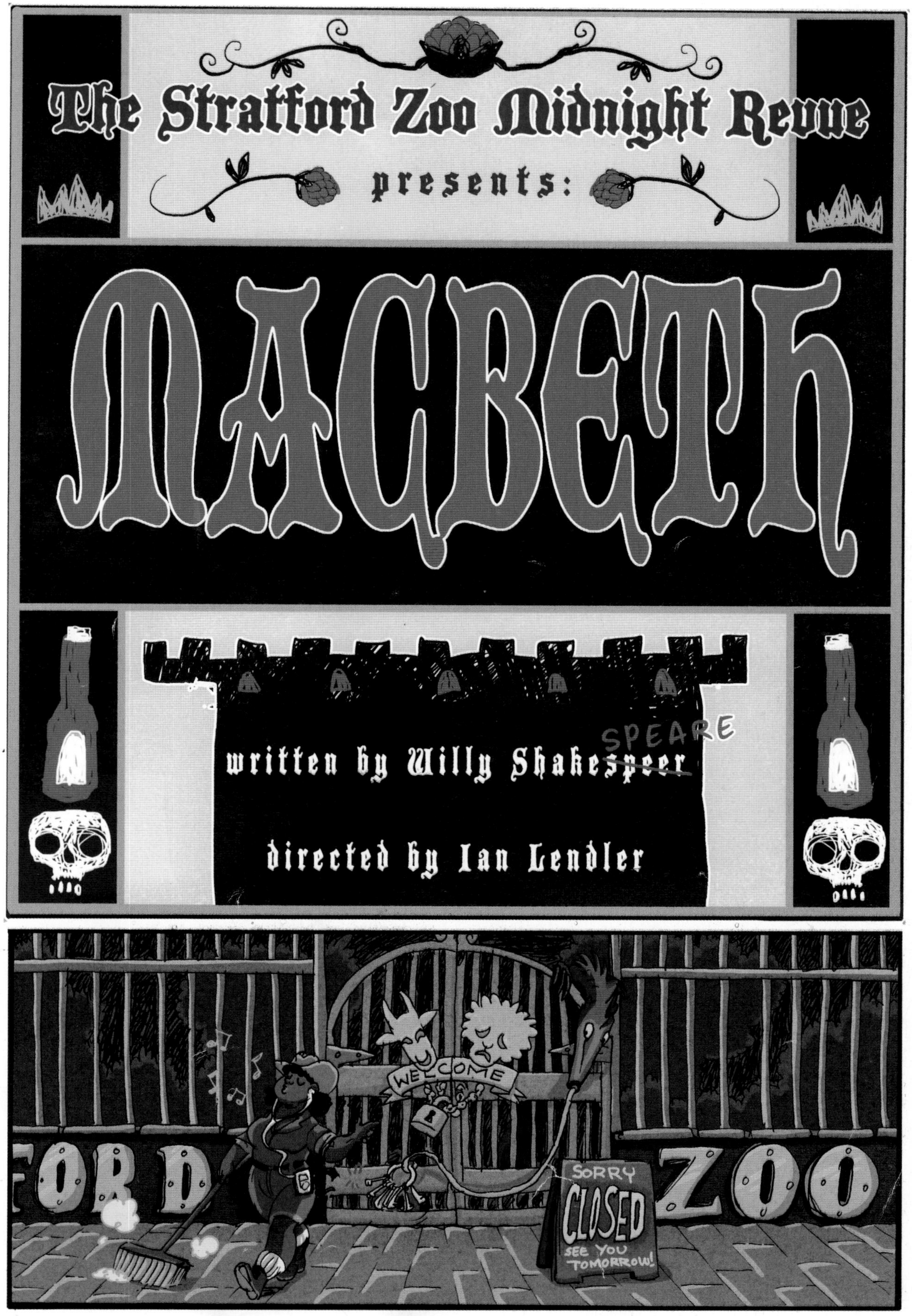
The Stratford Zoo Midnight Revue
presents:
MACBETH
written by Willy Shakespeer SPEARE
directed by Ian Lendler
WELCOME
ORD
ZOO
SORRY
CLOSED
SEE YOU TOMORROW!

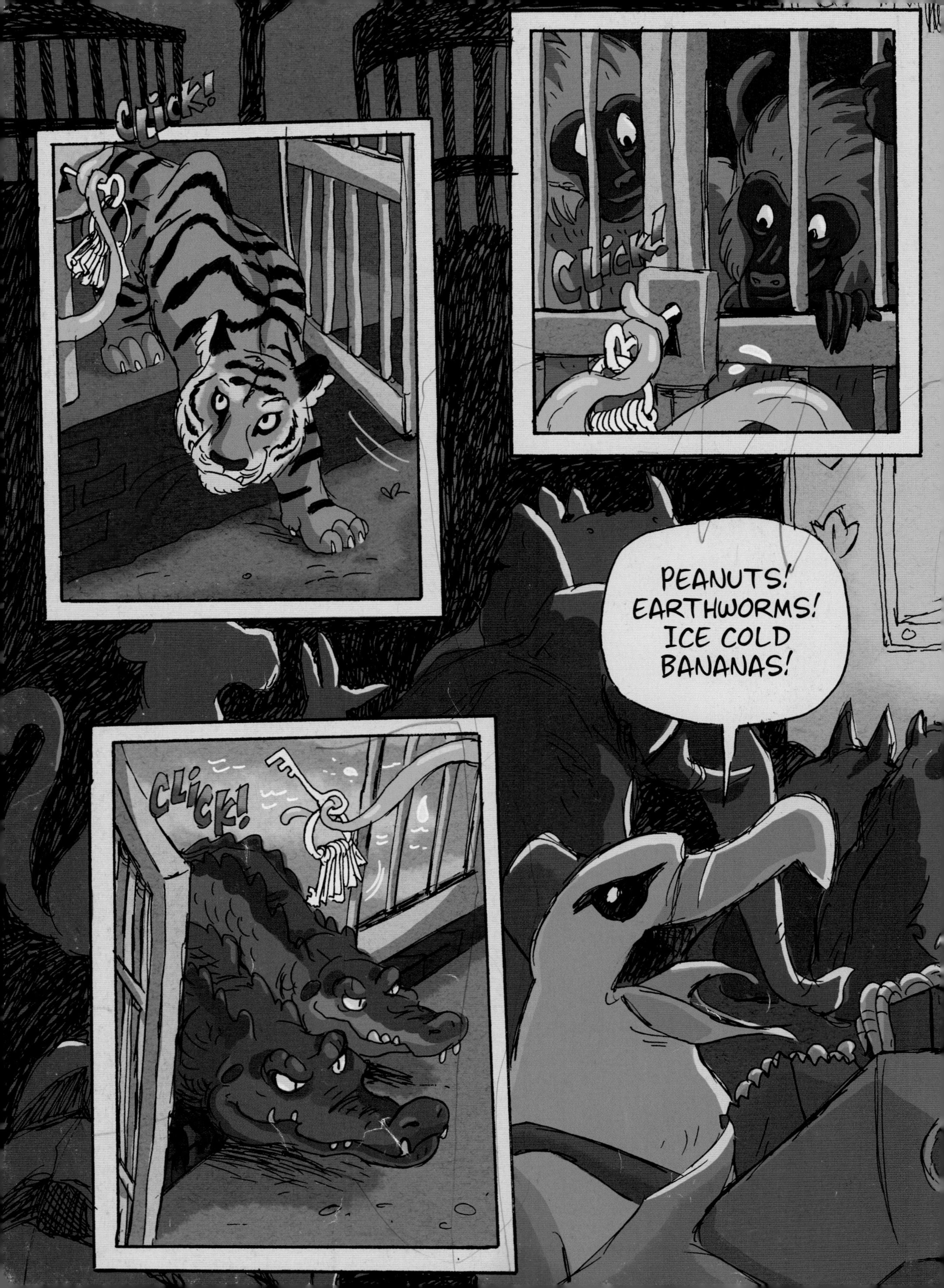
CLICK!
CLICK!
PEANUTS! EARTHWORMS! ICE COLD BANANAS!
CLICK!

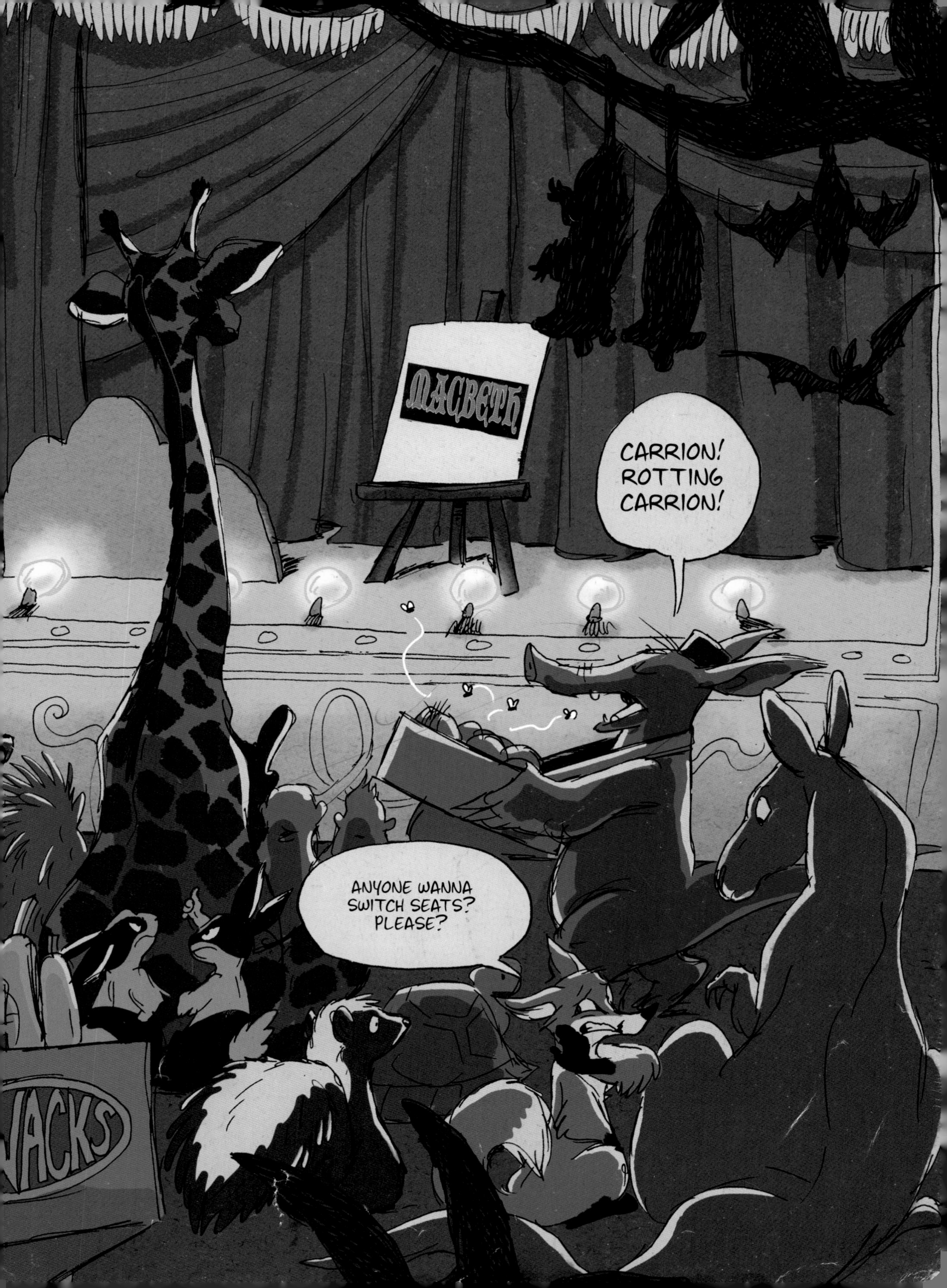
MACBETH
CARRION! ROTTING CARRION!
ANYONE WANNA SWITCH SEATS? PLEASE?
JACKS

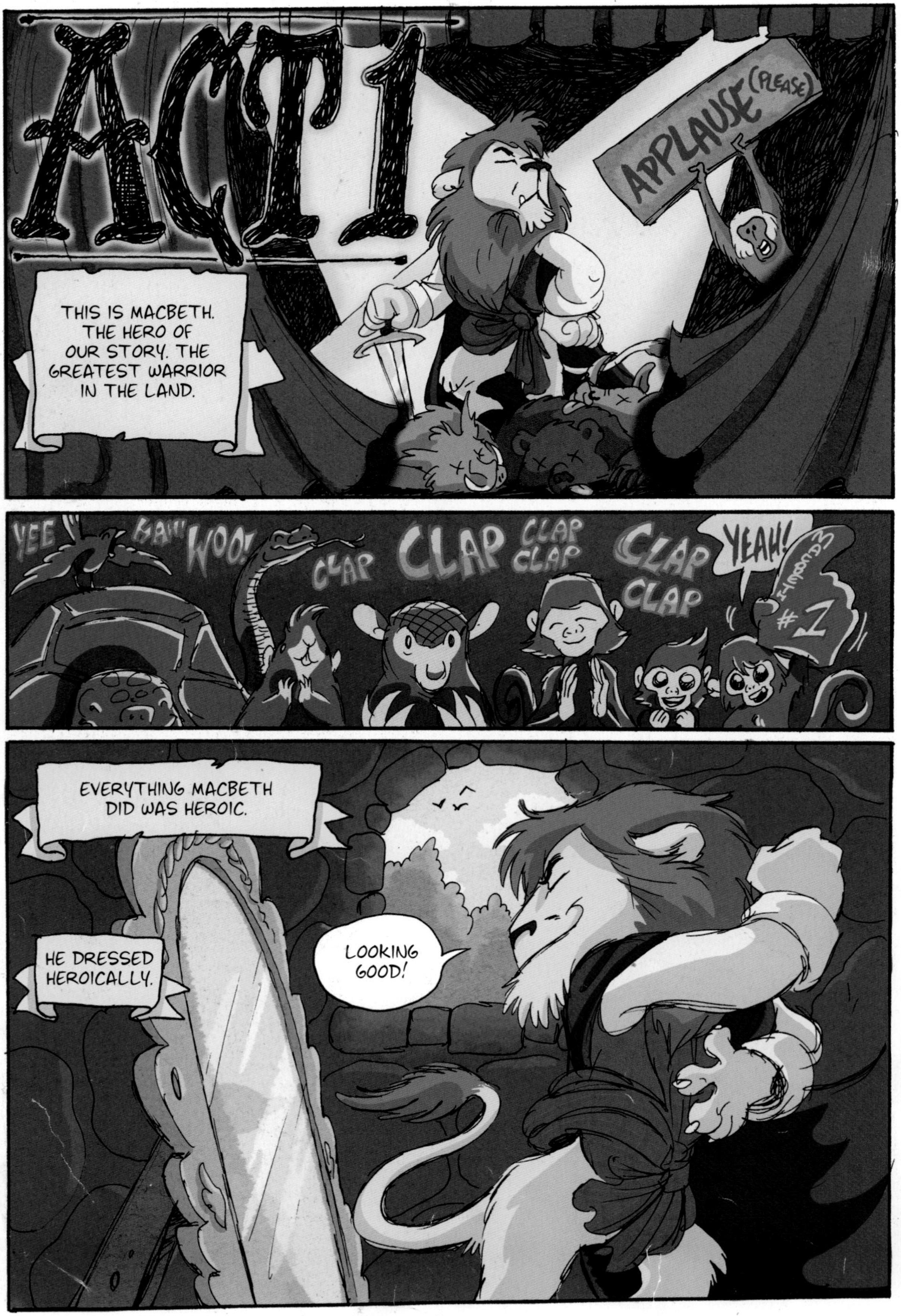
ACT 1
APPLAUSE (PLEASE)
THIS IS MACBETH. THE HERO OF OUR STORY. THE GREATEST WARRIOR IN THE LAND.
YEE HAW! WOO!
CLAP CLAP CLAP CLAP CLAP CLAP
YEAH!
#1
EVERYTHING MACBETH DID WAS HEROIC.
HE DRESSED HEROICALLY.
LOOKING GOOD!

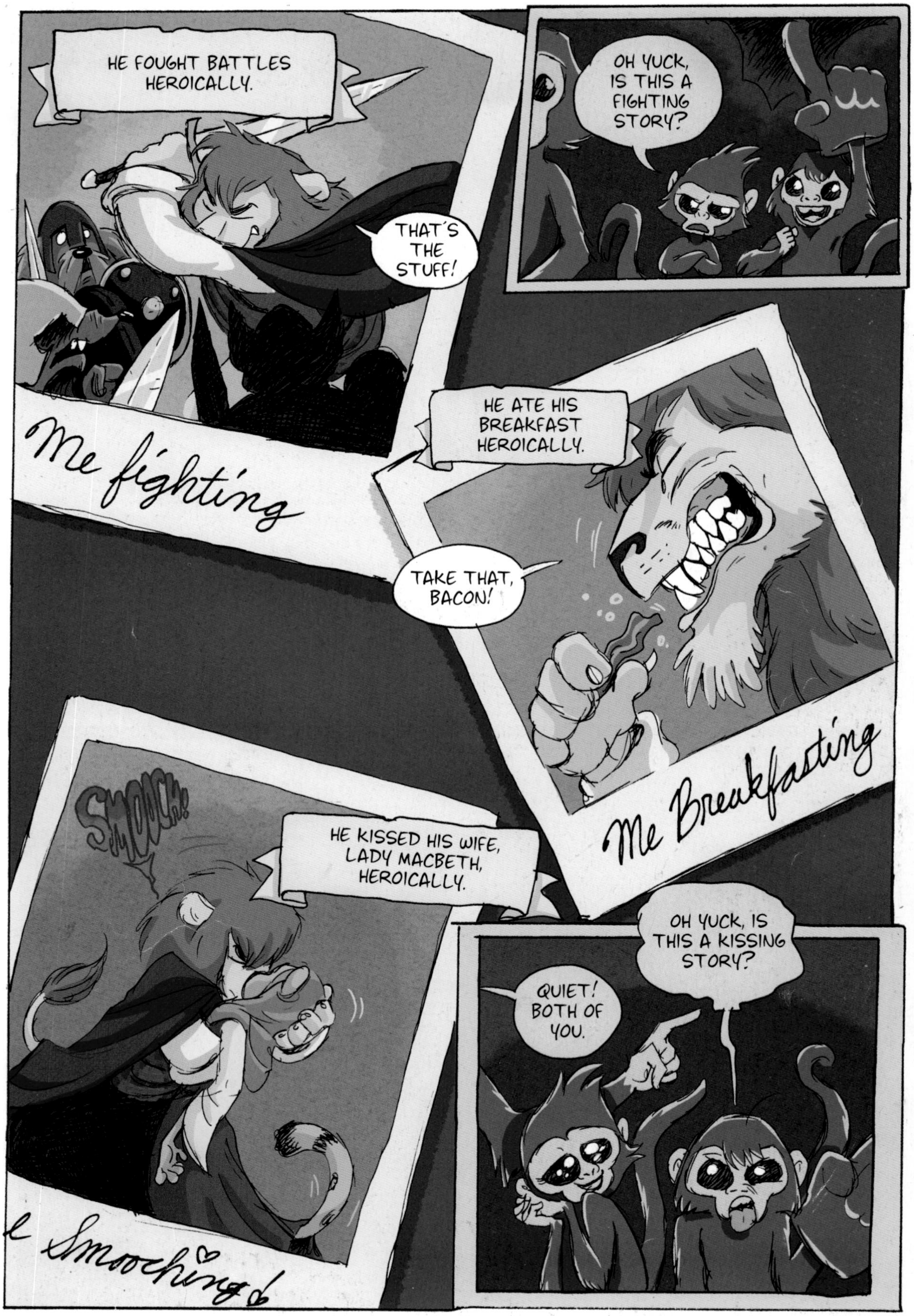
HE FOUGHT BATTLES HEROICALLY.
THAT'S THE STUFF!
Me fighting
OH YUCK, IS THIS A FIGHTING STORY?
HE ATE HIS BREAKFAST HEROICALLY.
TAKE THAT, BACON!
Me Breakfasting
SMOOCH!
HE KISSED HIS WIFE, LADY MACBETH, HEROICALLY.
& Smooching!
OH YUCK, IS THIS A KISSING STORY?
QUIET! BOTH OF YOU.

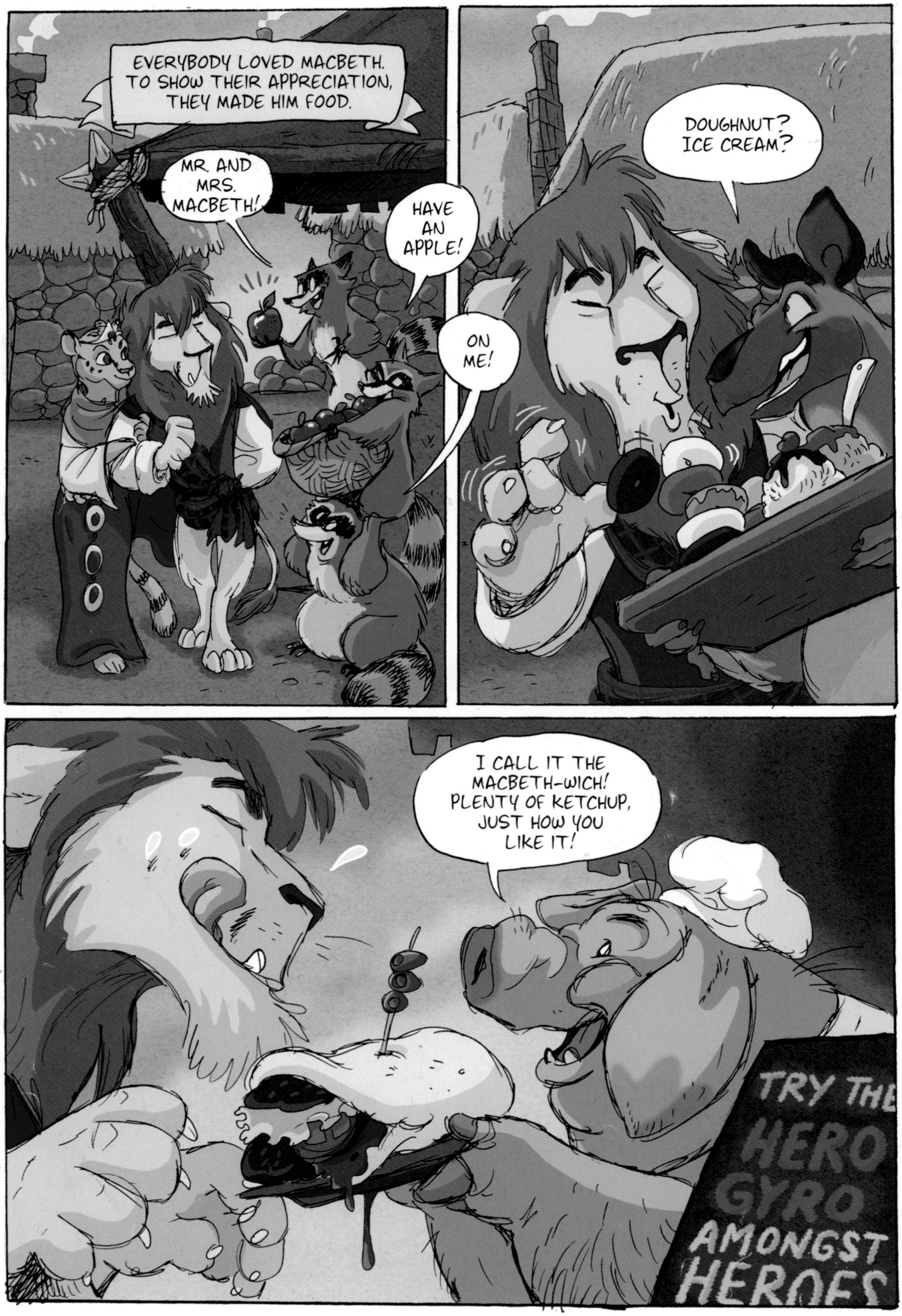
EVERYBODY LOVED MACBETH. TO SHOW THEIR APPRECIATION, THEY MADE HIM FOOD.
MR. AND MRS. MACBETH!
HAVE AN APPLE!
ON ME!
DOUGHNUT? ICE CREAM?
I CALL IT THE MACBETH-WICH! PLENTY OF KETCHUP, JUST HOW YOU LIKE IT!
TRY THE HERO GYRO AMONGST HEROES

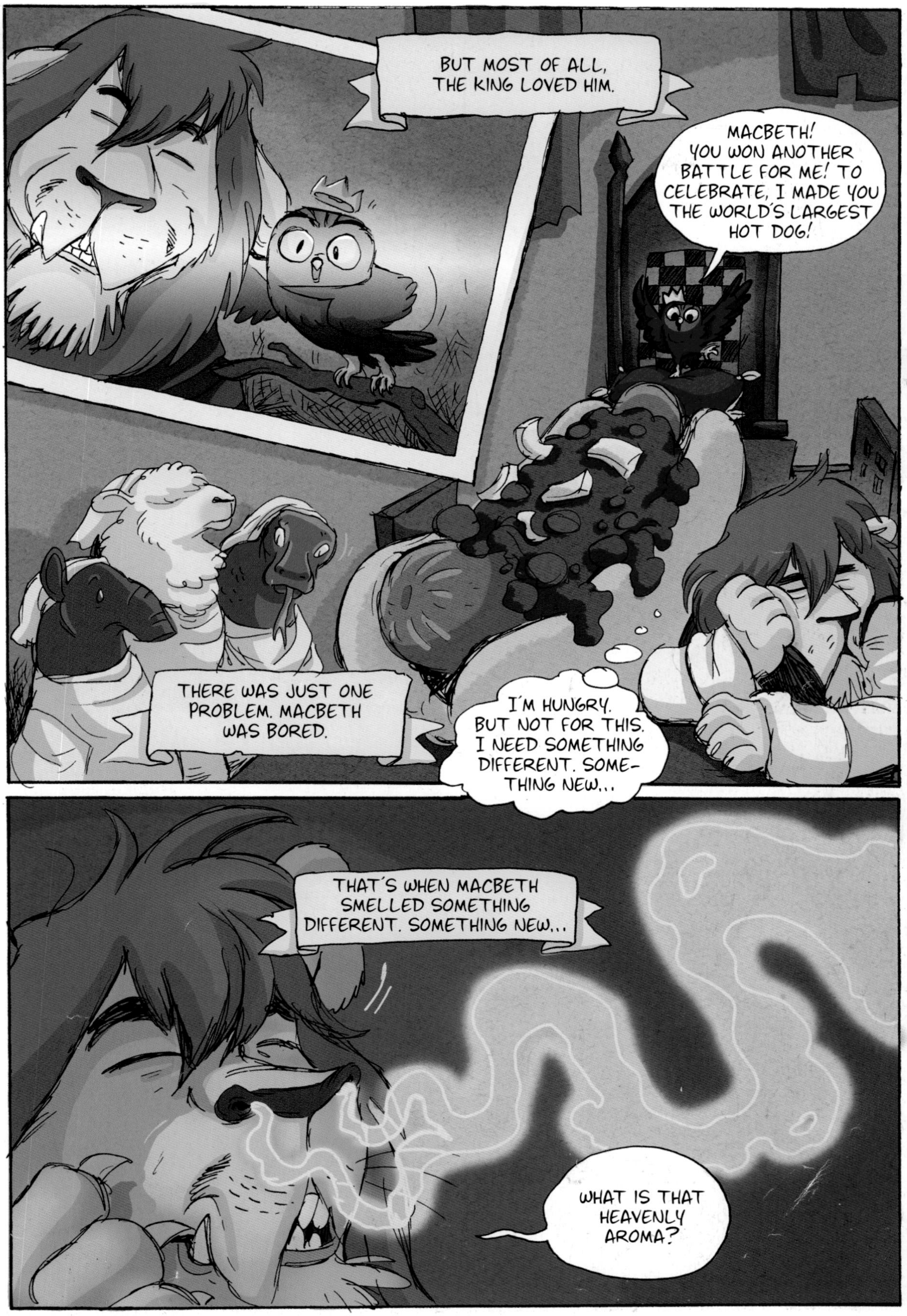
BUT MOST OF ALL, THE KING LOVED HIM.
MACBETH! YOU WON ANOTHER BATTLE FOR ME! TO CELEBRATE, I MADE YOU THE WORLD'S LARGEST HOT DOG!
THERE WAS JUST ONE PROBLEM. MACBETH WAS BORED.
I'M HUNGRY. BUT NOT FOR THIS. I NEED SOMETHING DIFFERENT. SOMETHING NEW...
THAT'S WHEN MACBETH SMELLED SOMETHING DIFFERENT. SOMETHING NEW...
WHAT IS THAT HEAVENLY AROMA?

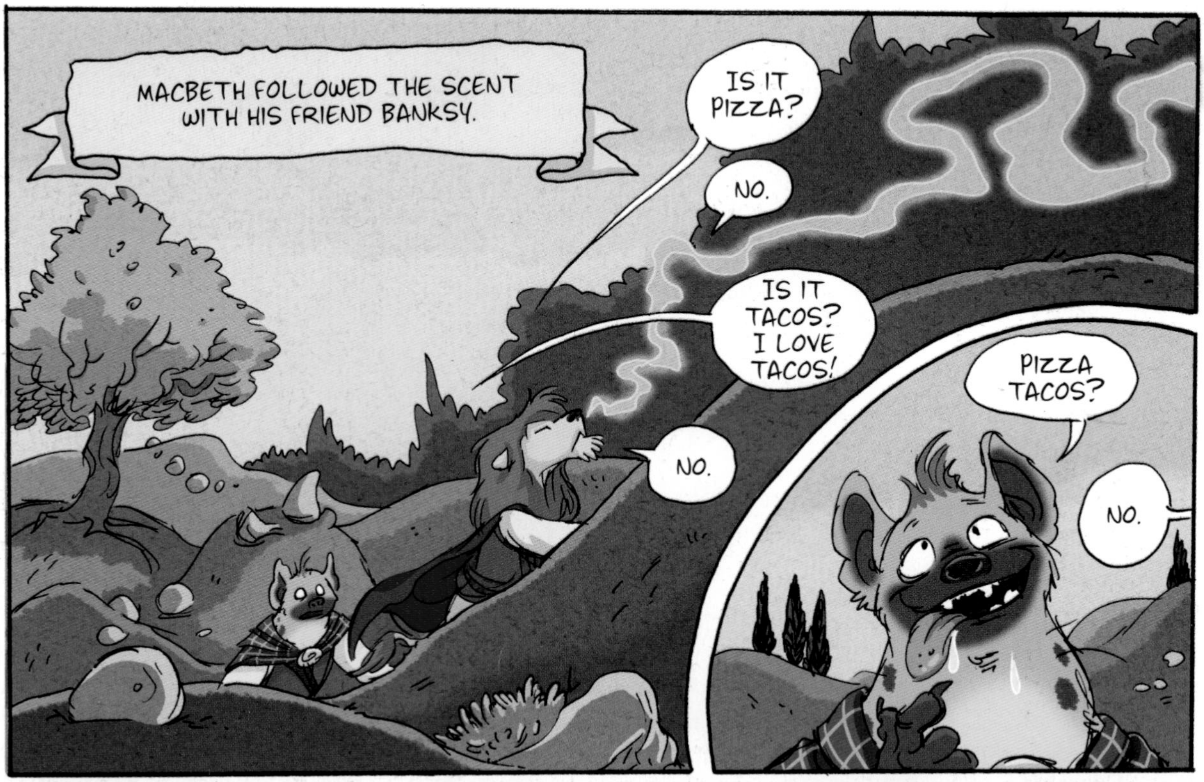

MACBETH FOLLOWED THE SCENT WITH HIS FRIEND BANKSY.
IS IT PIZZA?
NO.
IS IT TACOS? I LOVE TACOS!
NO.
PIZZA TACOS?
NO.

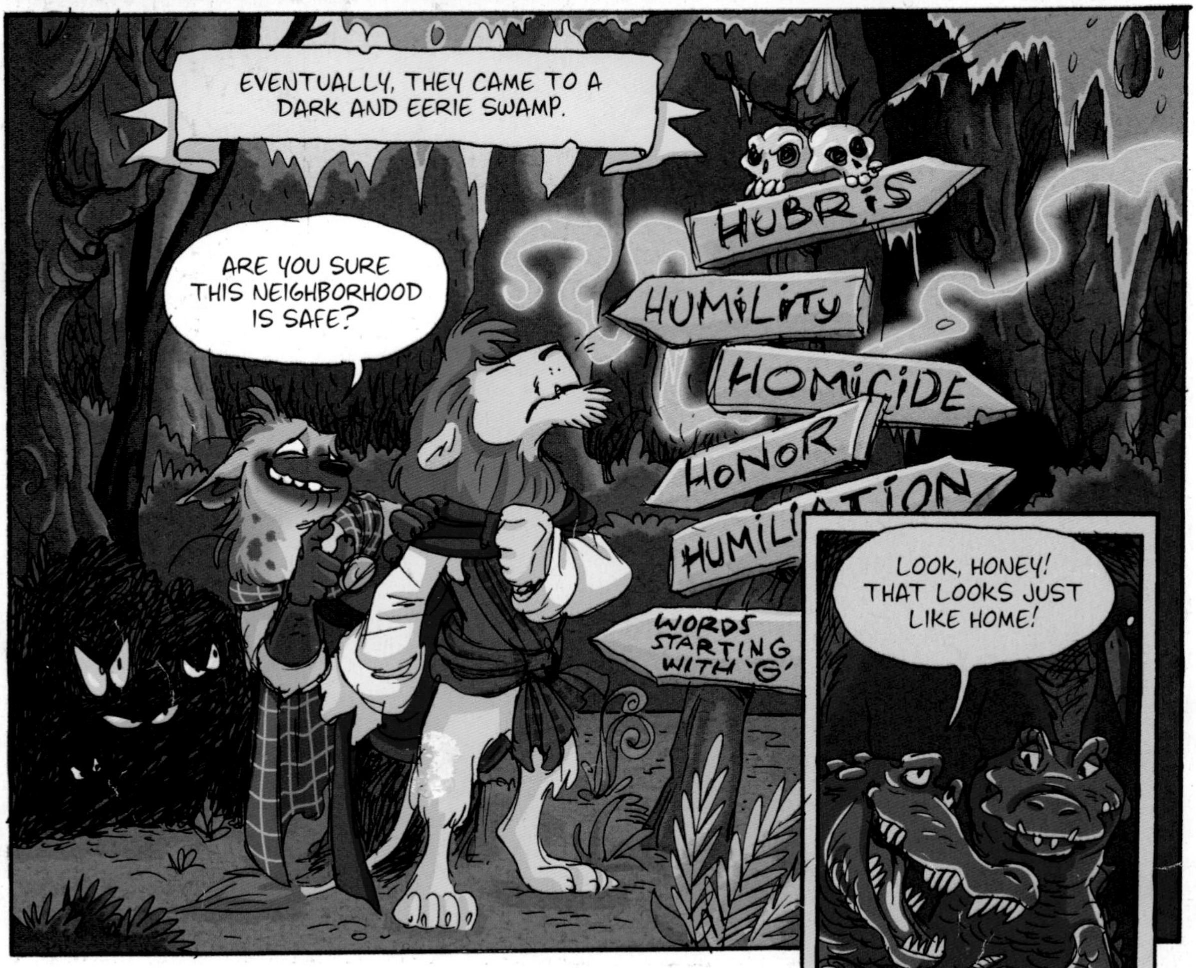

EVENTUALLY, THEY CAME TO A DARK AND EERIE SWAMP.
HUBRIS
HUMILITY
HOMICIDE
HONOR
HUMILIATION
WORDS STARTING WITH 'G'
ARE YOU SURE THIS NEIGHBORHOOD IS SAFE?
LOOK, HONEY! THAT LOOKS JUST LIKE HOME!

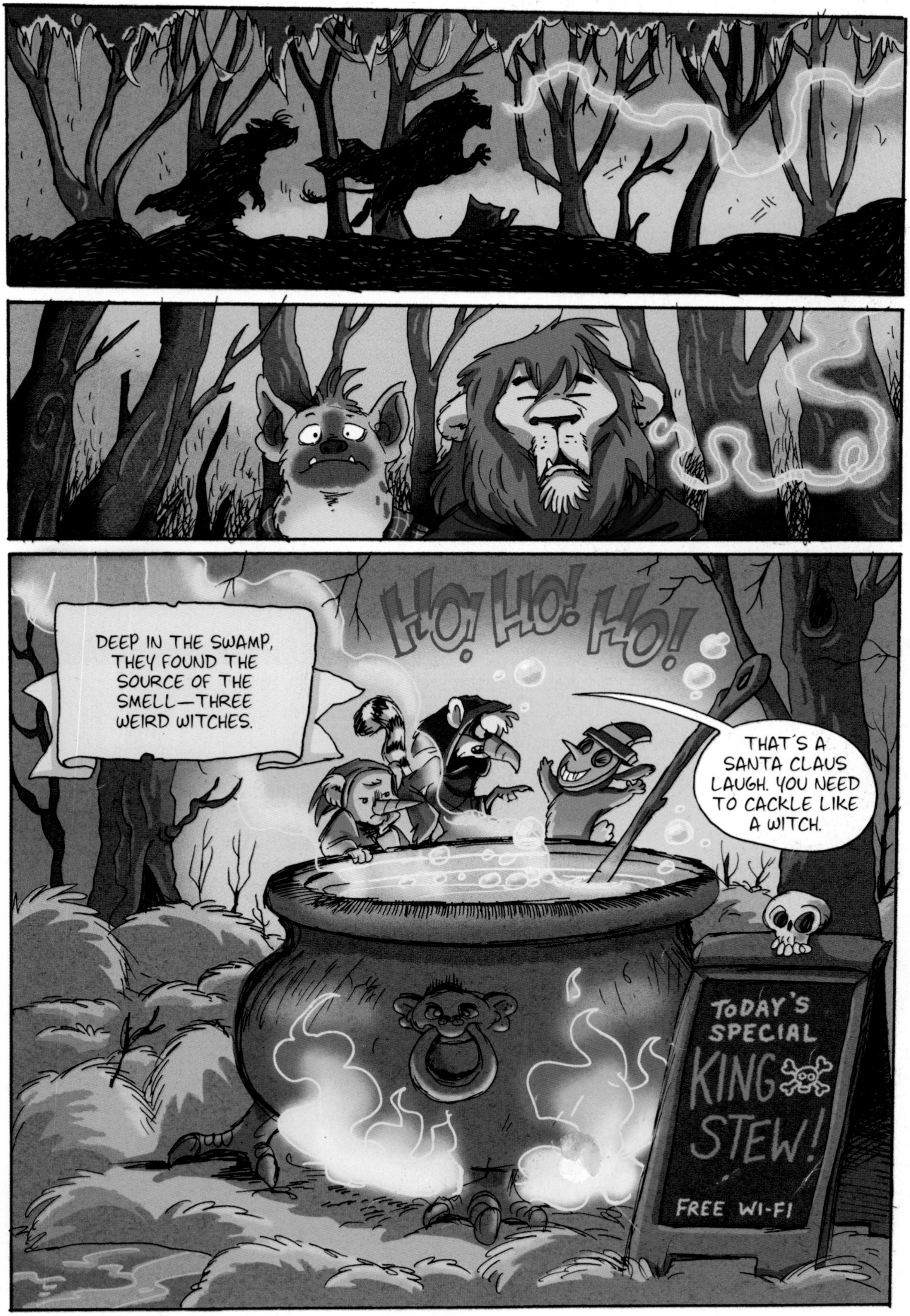
DEEP IN THE SWAMP, THEY FOUND THE SOURCE OF THE SMELL—THREE WEIRD WITCHES.
HO! HO! HO!
THAT´S A SANTA CLAUS LAUGH. YOU NEED TO CACKLE LIKE A WITCH.
TODAY´S SPECIAL
KING STEW!
FREE WI-FI

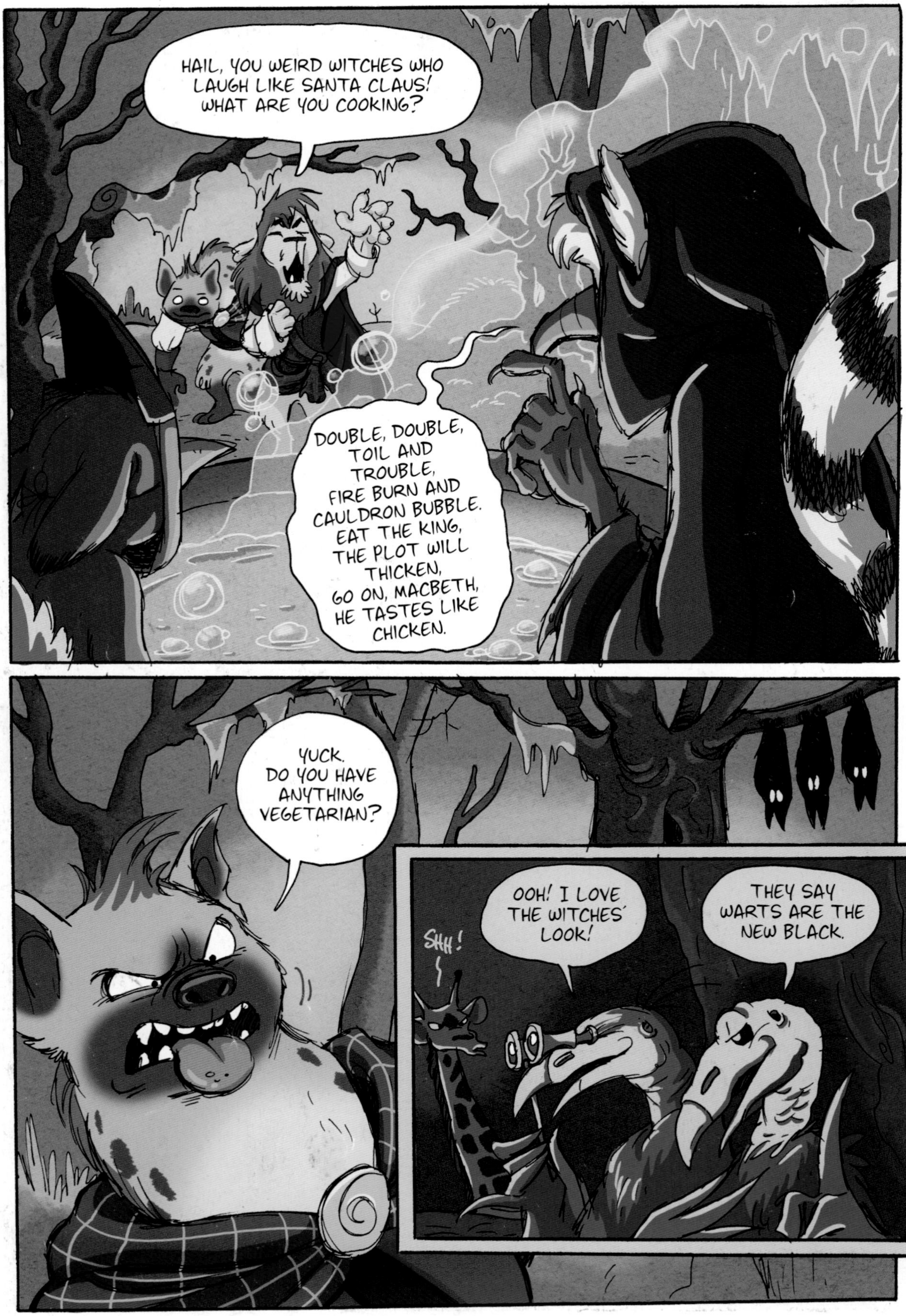
HAIL, YOU WEIRD WITCHES WHO LAUGH LIKE SANTA CLAUS! WHAT ARE YOU COOKING?
DOUBLE, DOUBLE, TOIL AND TROUBLE, FIRE BURN AND CAULDRON BUBBLE. EAT THE KING, THE PLOT WILL THICKEN, GO ON, MACBETH, HE TASTES LIKE CHICKEN.
YUCK. DO YOU HAVE ANYTHING VEGETARIAN?
SHH!
OOH! I LOVE THE WITCHES' LOOK!
THEY SAY WARTS ARE THE NEW BLACK.

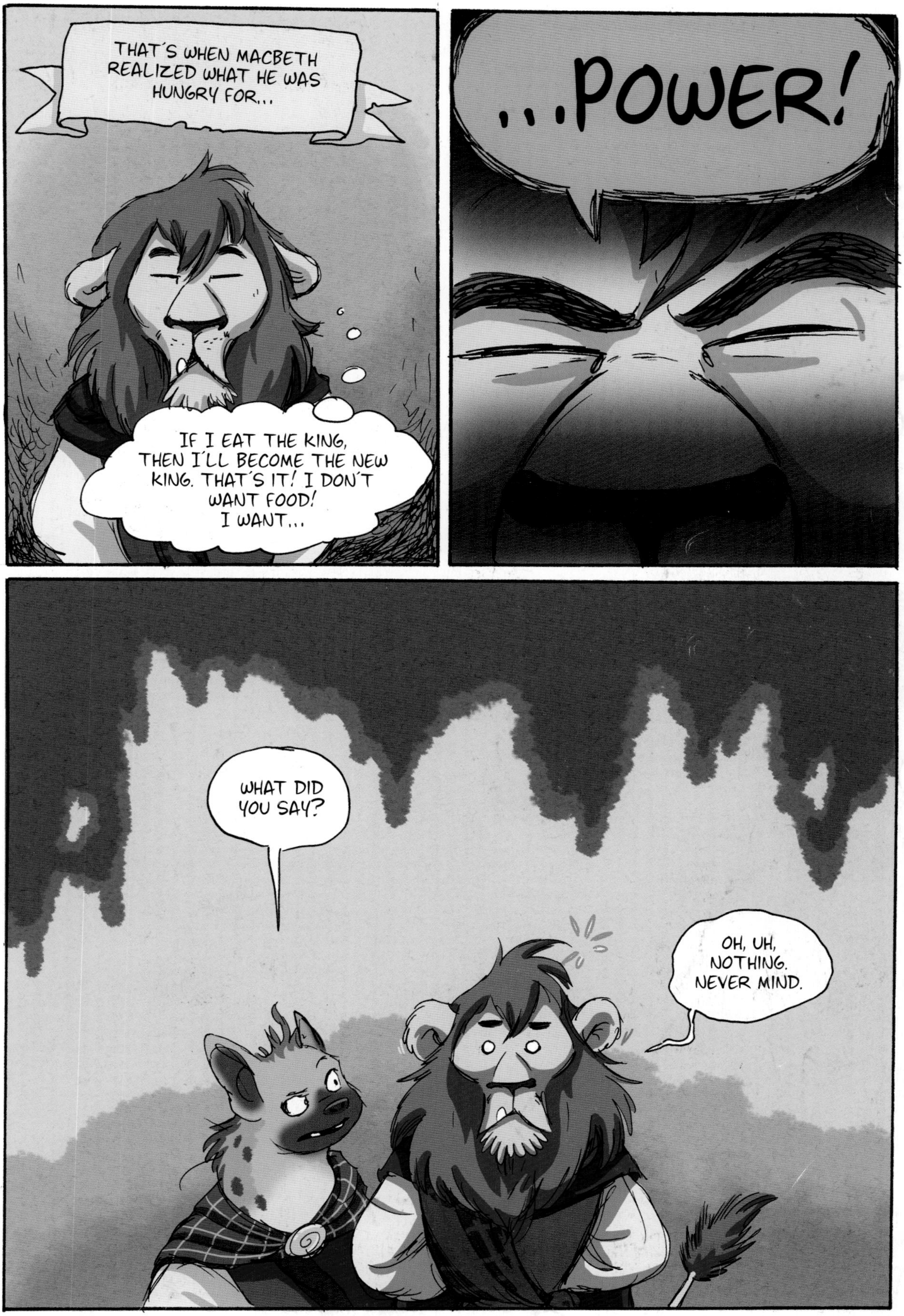
THAT´S WHEN MACBETH REALIZED WHAT HE WAS HUNGRY FOR...
IF I EAT THE KING, THEN I´LL BECOME THE NEW KING. THAT´S IT! I DON´T WANT FOOD! I WANT...
...POWER!
WHAT DID YOU SAY?
OH, UH, NOTHING. NEVER MIND.

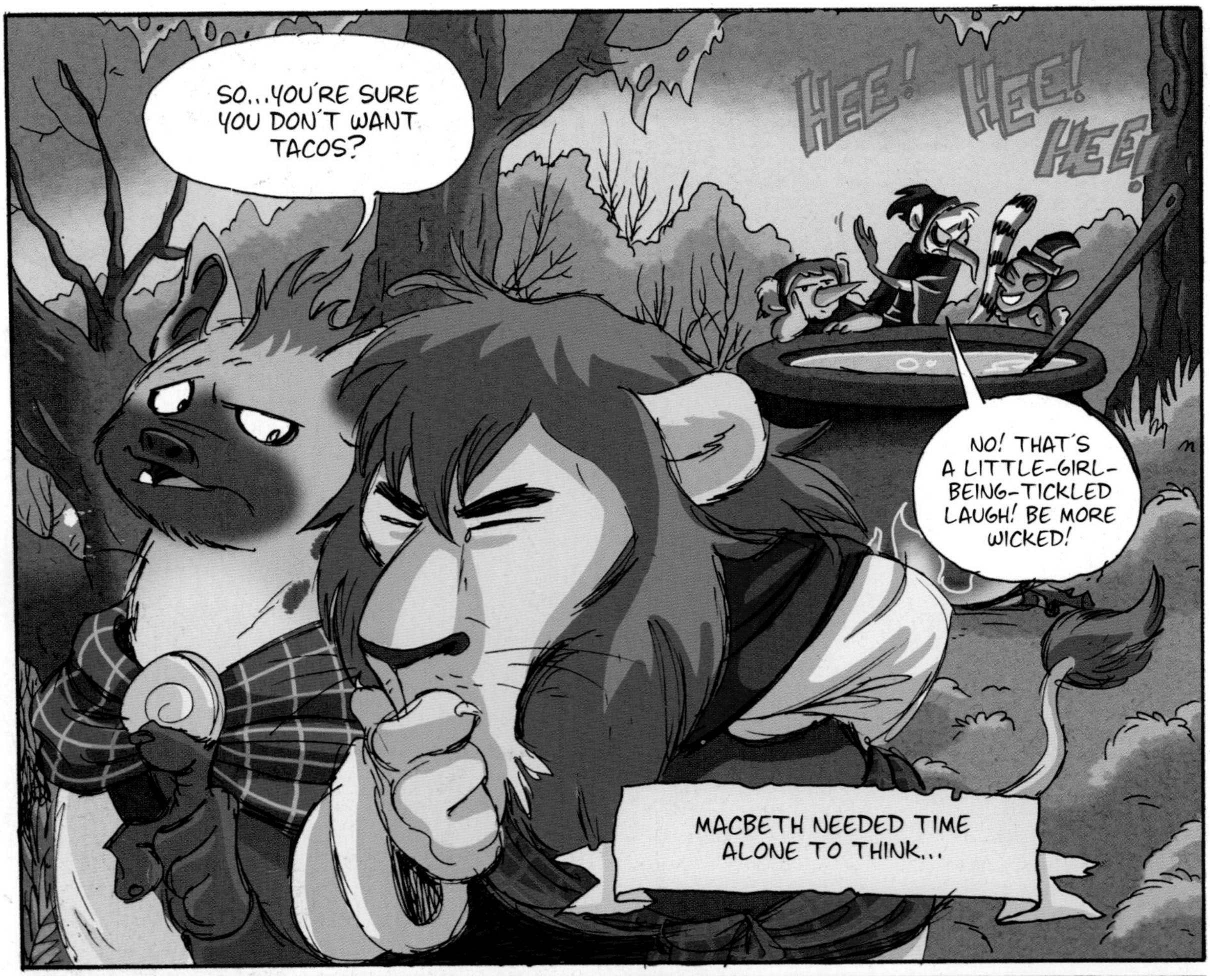
SO...YOU'RE SURE YOU DON'T WANT TACOS?
HEE! HEE! HEE!
NO! THAT'S A LITTLE-GIRL-BEING-TICKLED LAUGH! BE MORE WICKED!
MACBETH NEEDED TIME ALONE TO THINK...

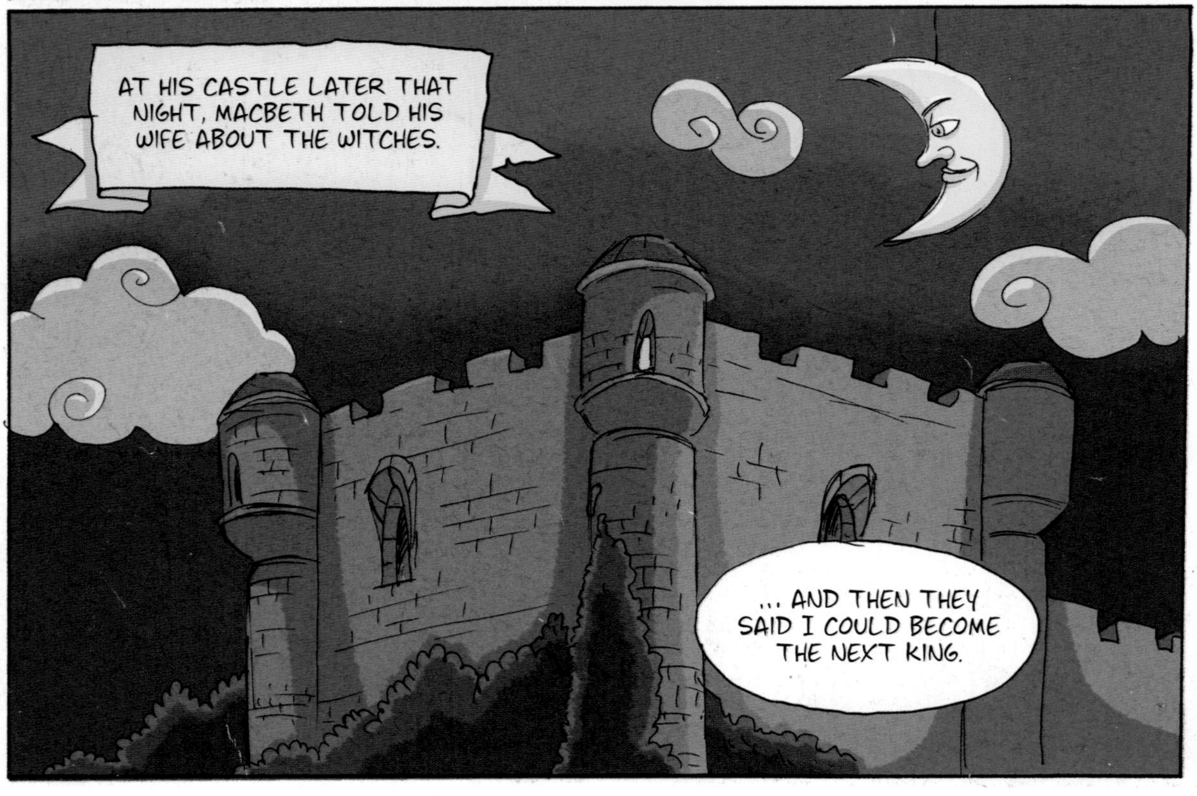
AT HIS CASTLE LATER THAT NIGHT, MACBETH TOLD HIS WIFE ABOUT THE WITCHES.
... AND THEN THEY SAID I COULD BECOME THE NEXT KING.

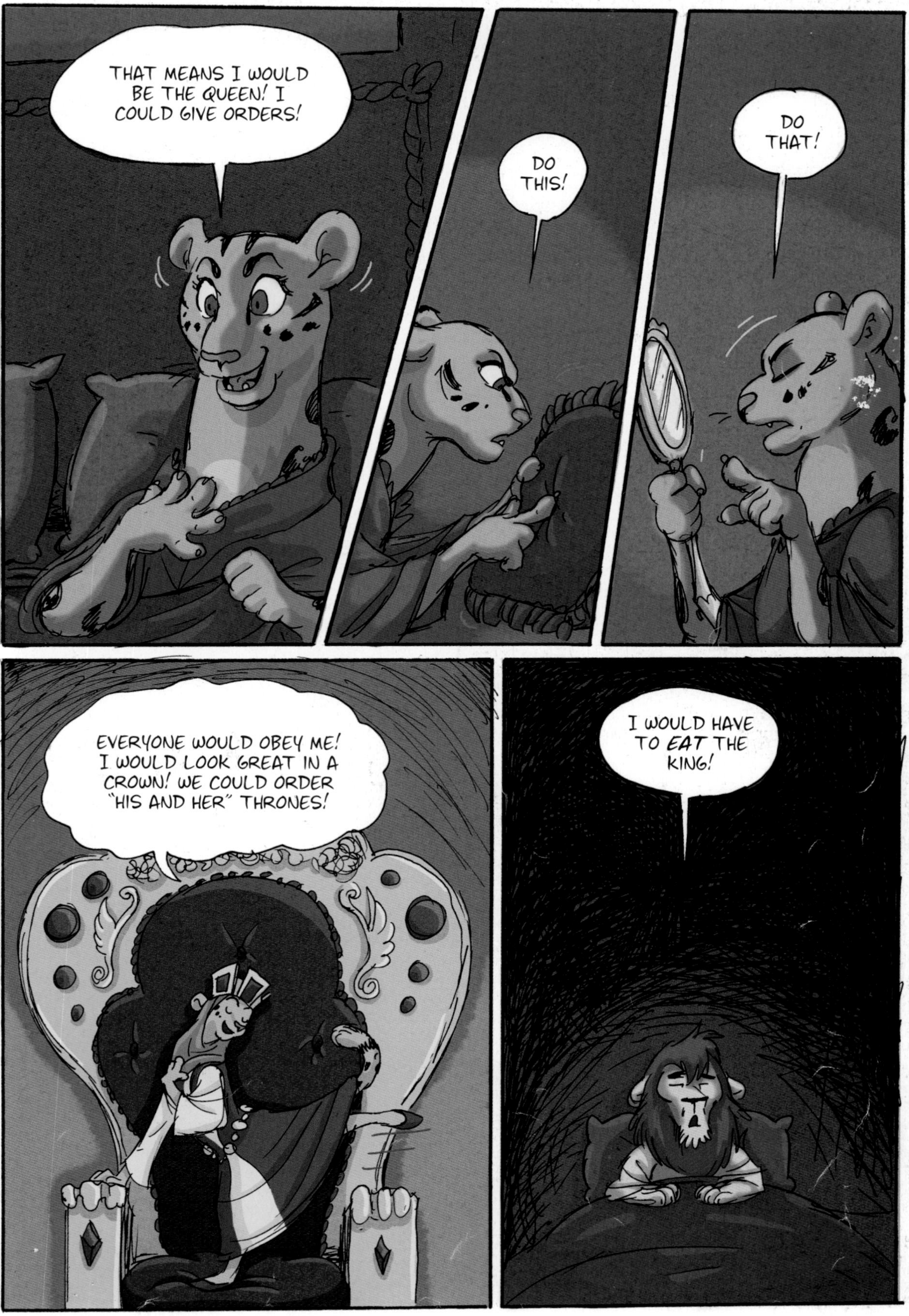
THAT MEANS I WOULD BE THE QUEEN! I COULD GIVE ORDERS!
DO THIS!
DO THAT!
EVERYONE WOULD OBEY ME! I WOULD LOOK GREAT IN A CROWN! WE COULD ORDER "HIS AND HER" THRONES!
I WOULD HAVE TO *EAT* THE KING!

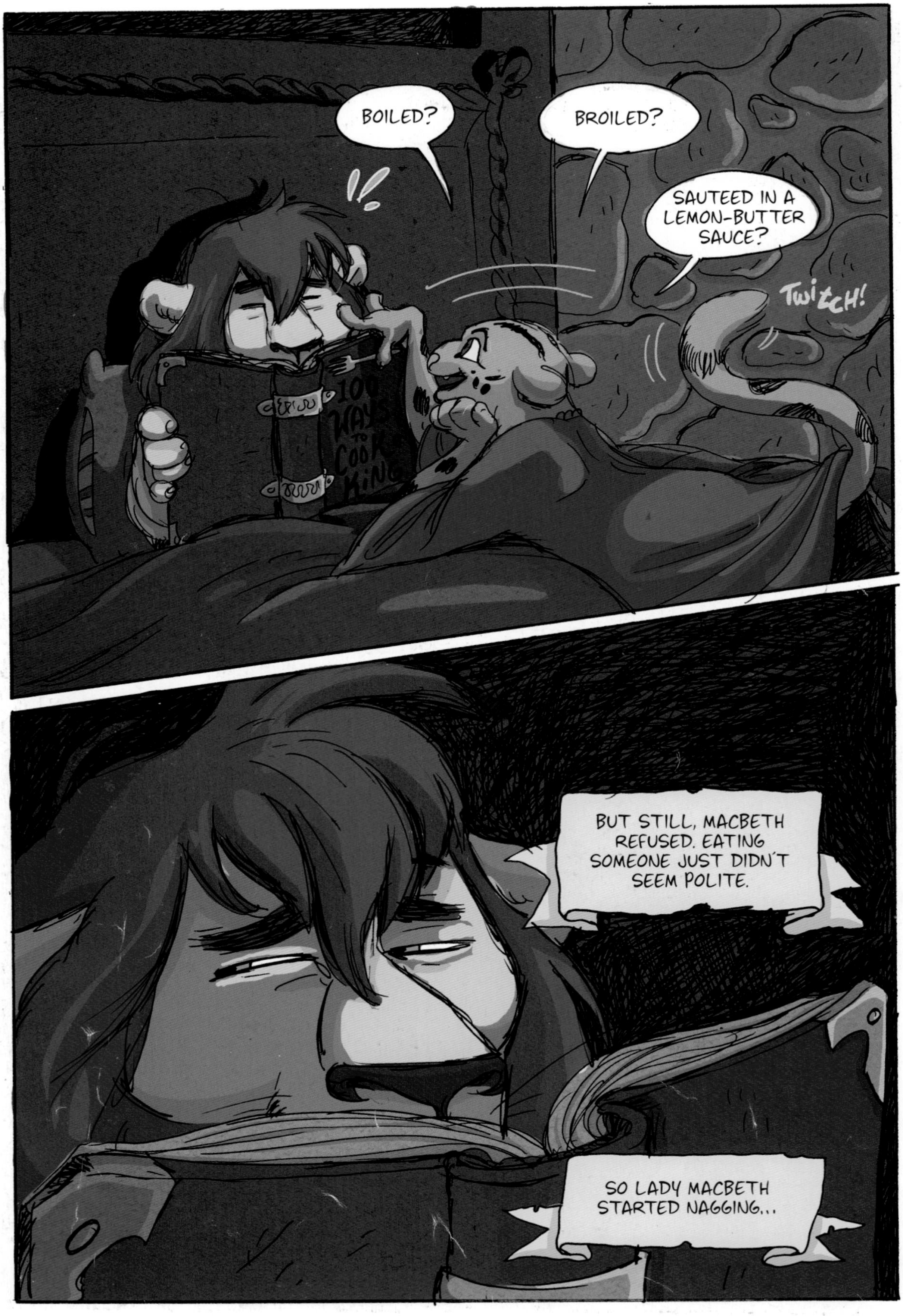
BOILED?
BROILED?
SAUTEED IN A LEMON-BUTTER SAUCE?
TWITCH!
100 WAYS TO COOK KING
BUT STILL, MACBETH REFUSED. EATING SOMEONE JUST DIDN'T SEEM POLITE.
SO LADY MACBETH STARTED NAGGING...

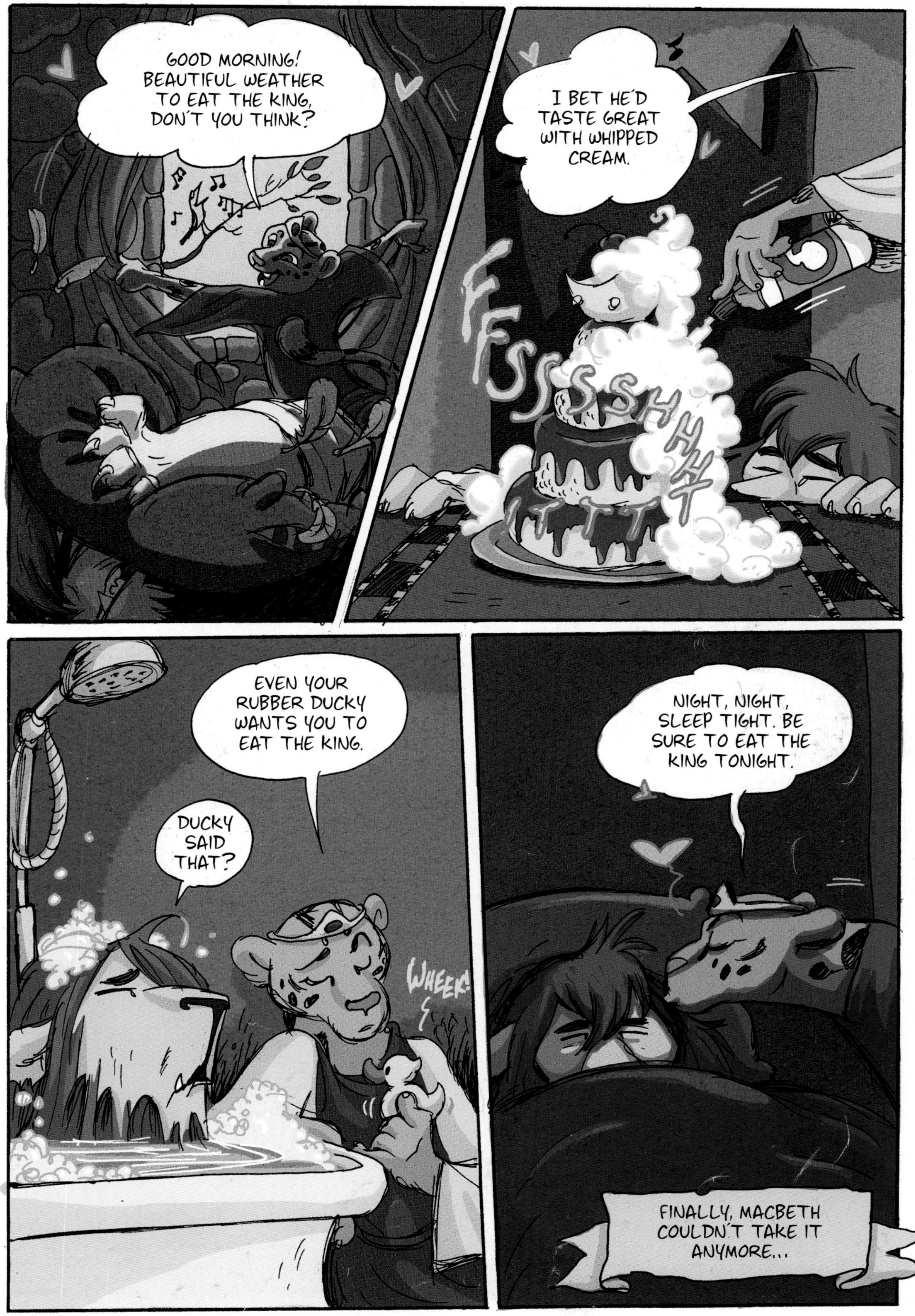
GOOD MORNING! BEAUTIFUL WEATHER TO EAT THE KING, DON'T YOU THINK?
I BET HE'D TASTE GREAT WITH WHIPPED CREAM.
FFSSSSHHHH
EVEN YOUR RUBBER DUCKY WANTS YOU TO EAT THE KING.
DUCKY SAID THAT?
WHEEK!
NIGHT, NIGHT, SLEEP TIGHT. BE SURE TO EAT THE KING TONIGHT.
FINALLY, MACBETH COULDN'T TAKE IT ANYMORE...

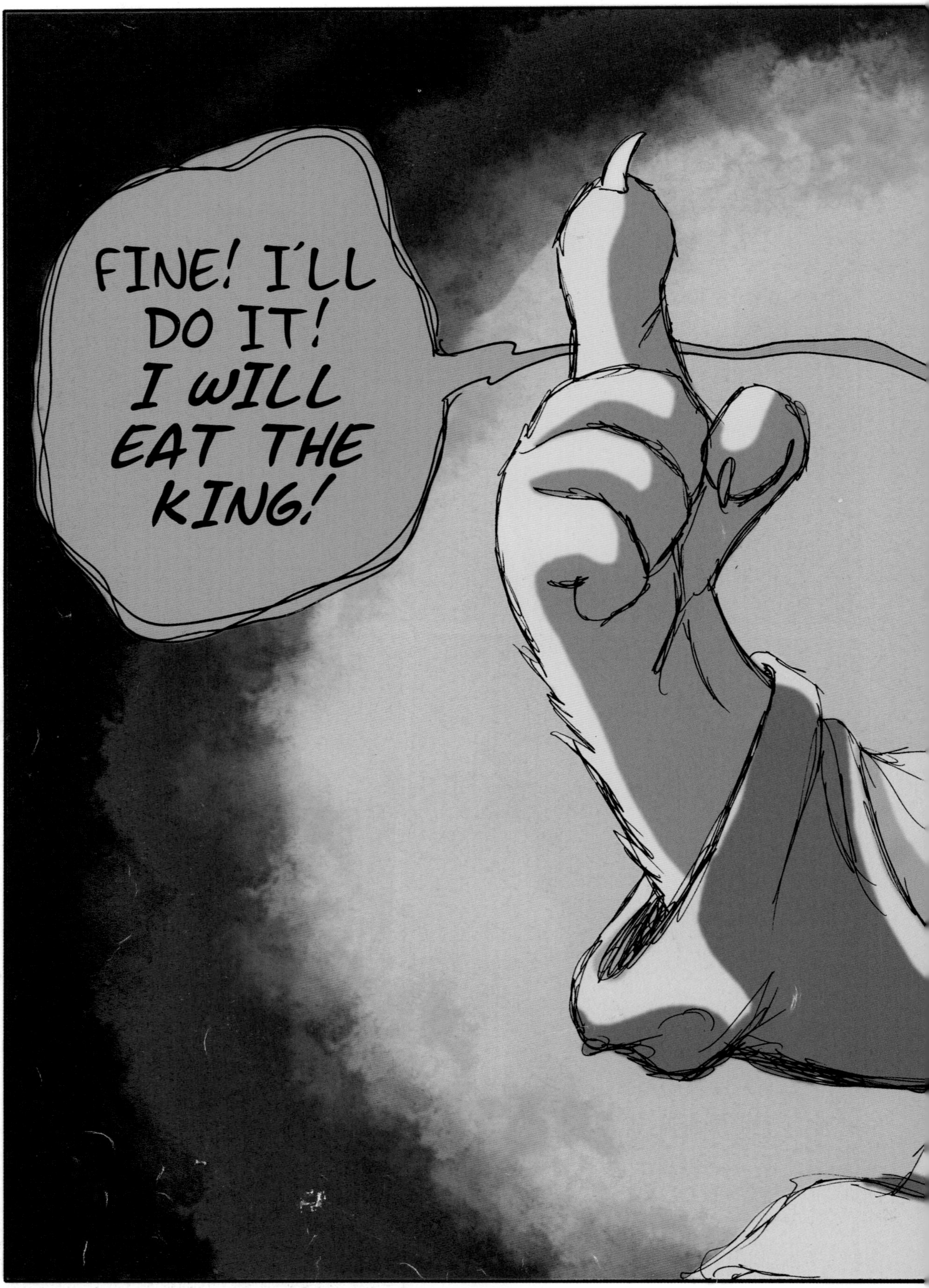
FINE! I'LL DO IT! I WILL EAT THE KING!

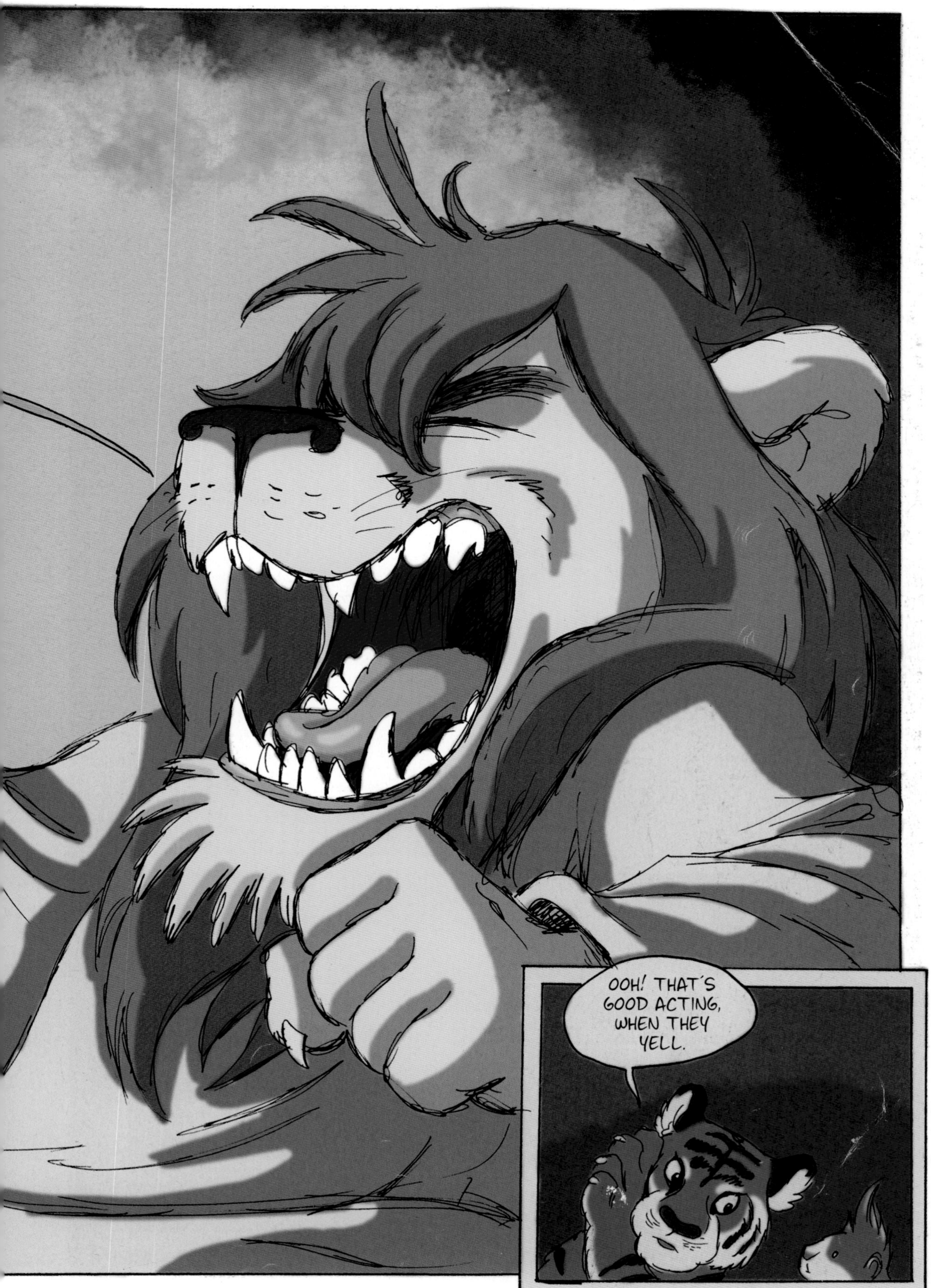
OOH! THAT'S GOOD ACTING, WHEN THEY YELL.

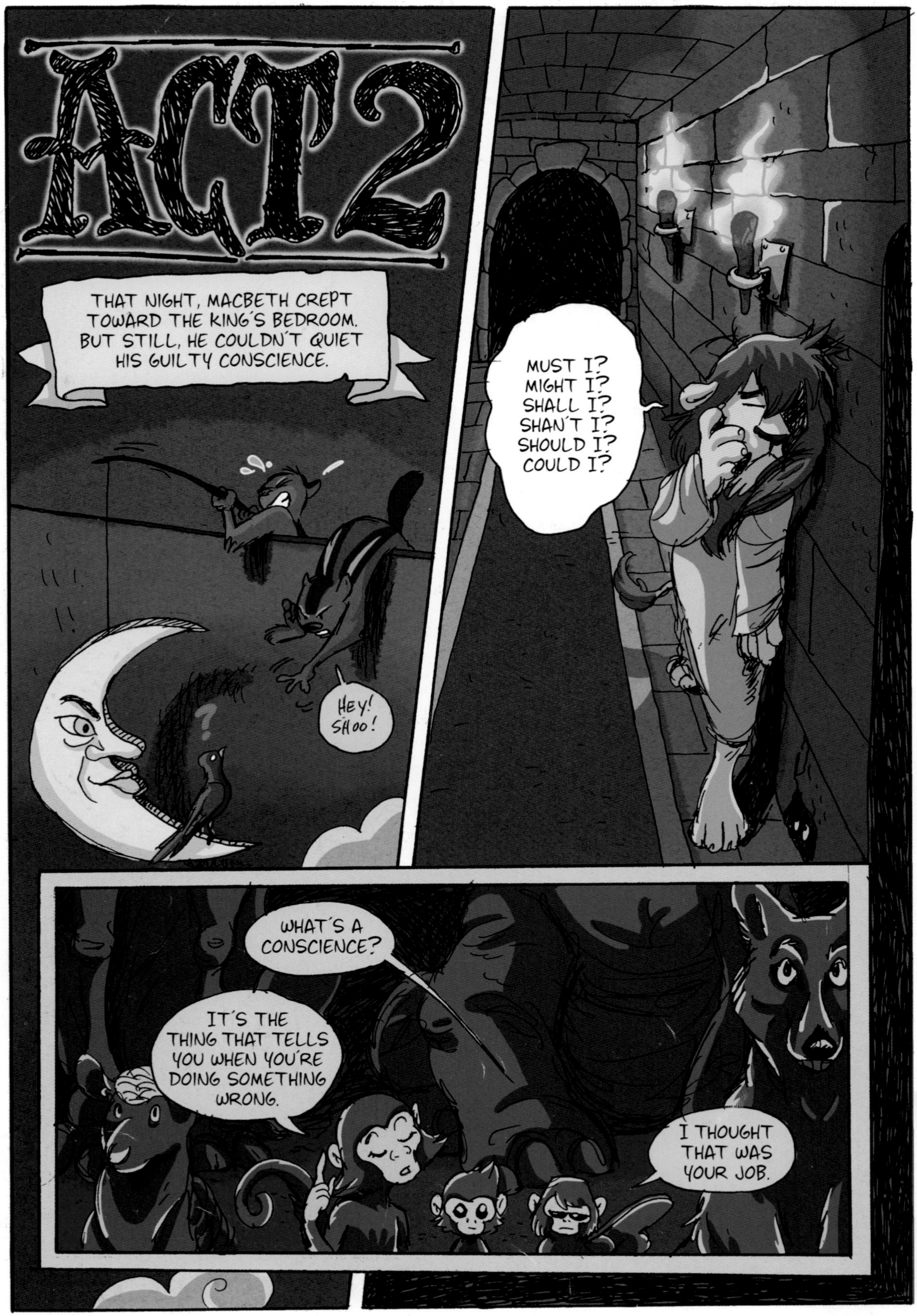
ACT 2
THAT NIGHT, MACBETH CREPT TOWARD THE KING'S BEDROOM. BUT STILL, HE COULDN'T QUIET HIS GUILTY CONSCIENCE.
HEY! SHOO!
MUST I? MIGHT I? SHALL I? SHAN'T I? SHOULD I? COULD I?
WHAT'S A CONSCIENCE?
IT'S THE THING THAT TELLS YOU WHEN YOU'RE DOING SOMETHING WRONG.
I THOUGHT THAT WAS YOUR JOB.

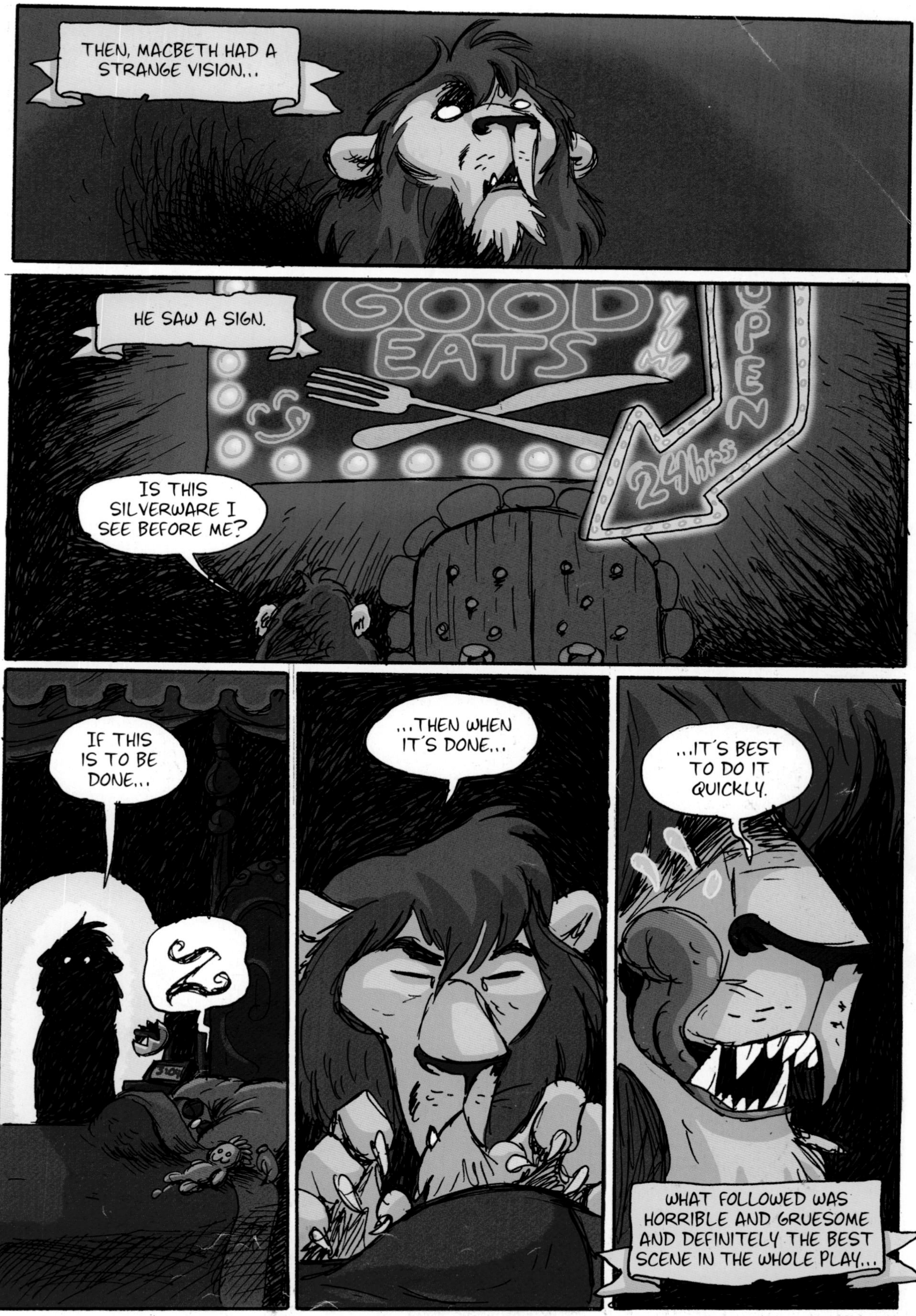
THEN, MACBETH HAD A STRANGE VISION...
HE SAW A SIGN.
GOOD EATS
OPEN
24hrs
IS THIS SILVERWARE I SEE BEFORE ME?
IF THIS IS TO BE DONE...
...THEN WHEN IT'S DONE...
...IT'S BEST TO DO IT QUICKLY.
WHAT FOLLOWED WAS HORRIBLE AND GRUESOME AND DEFINITELY THE BEST SCENE IN THE WHOLE PLAY...

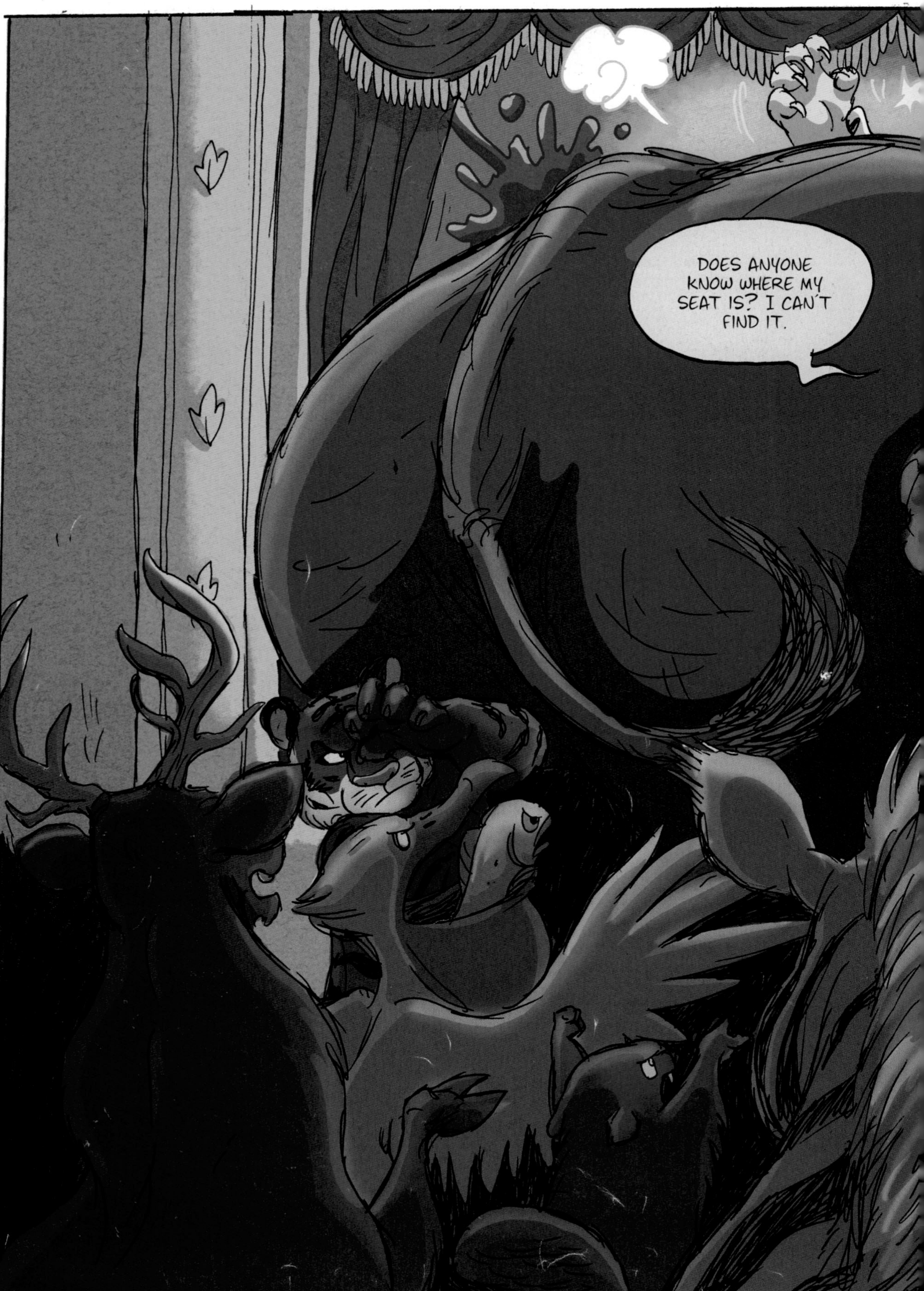
DOES ANYONE KNOW WHERE MY SEAT IS? I CAN'T FIND IT.

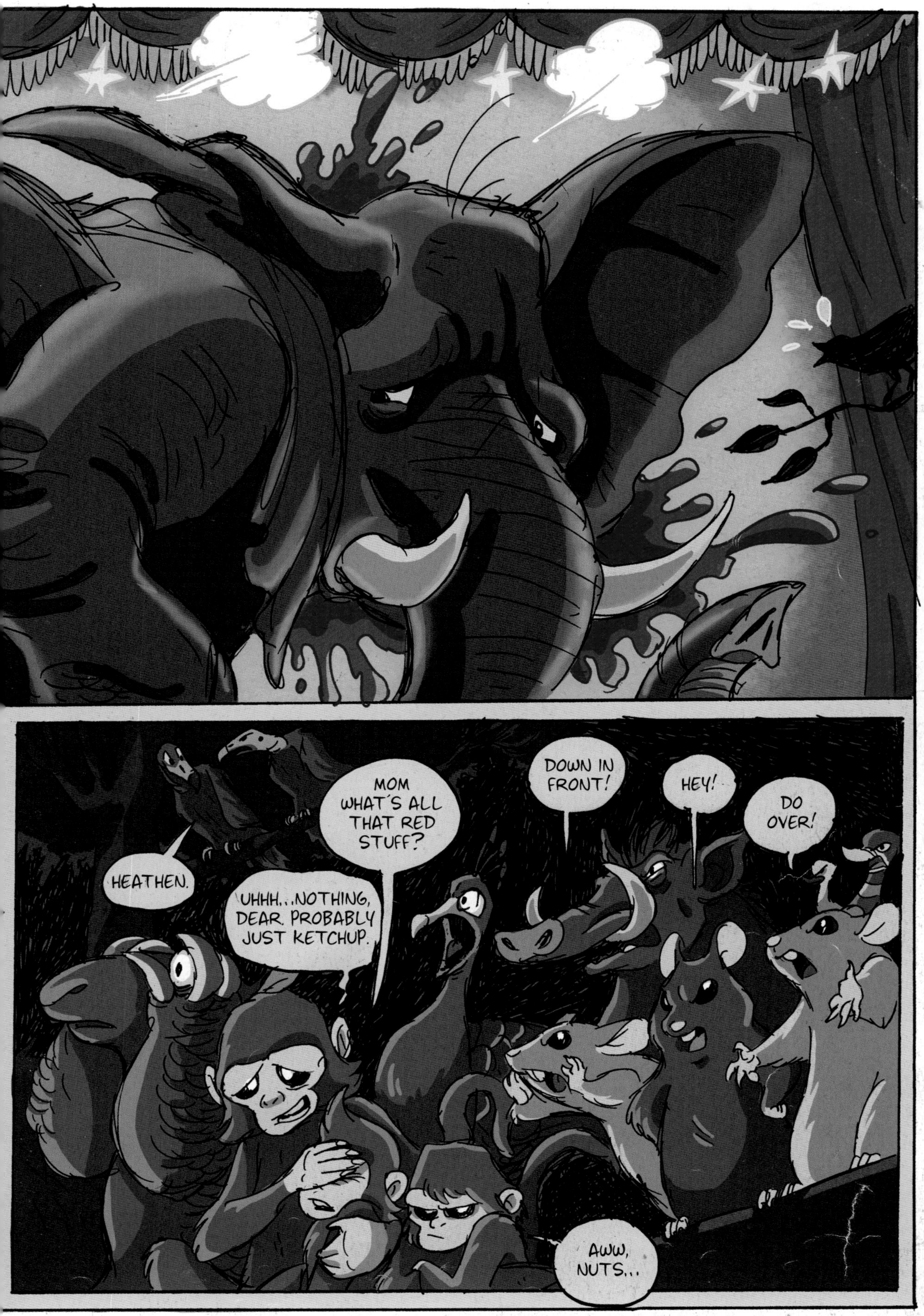
HEATHEN.
MOM WHAT'S ALL THAT RED STUFF?
UHHH...NOTHING, DEAR. PROBABLY JUST KETCHUP.
DOWN IN FRONT!
HEY!
DO OVER!
AWW, NUTS...

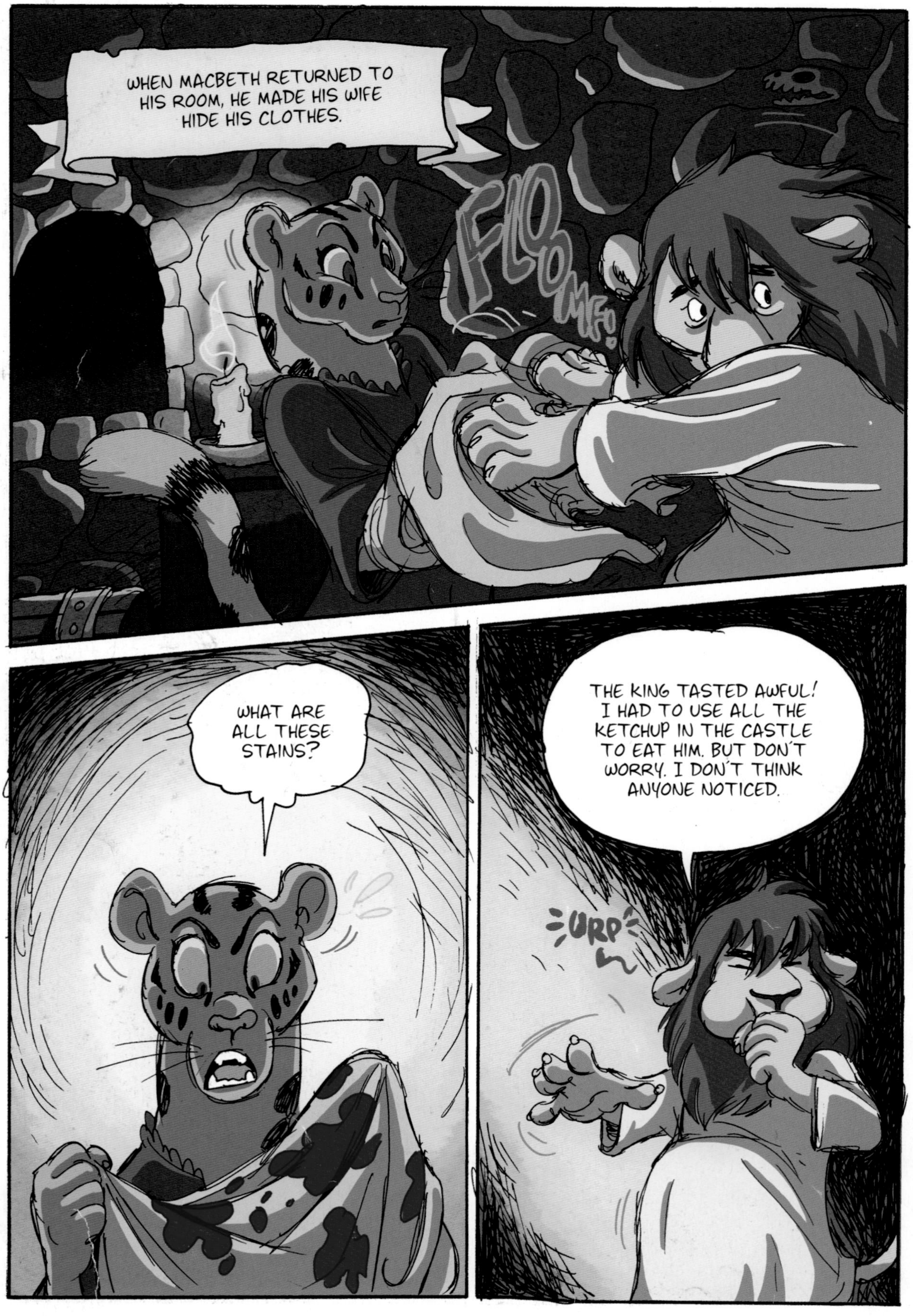
WHEN MACBETH RETURNED TO HIS ROOM, HE MADE HIS WIFE HIDE HIS CLOTHES.
FLOOMF!
WHAT ARE ALL THESE STAINS?
THE KING TASTED AWFUL! I HAD TO USE ALL THE KETCHUP IN THE CASTLE TO EAT HIM. BUT DON'T WORRY. I DON'T THINK ANYONE NOTICED.
URP

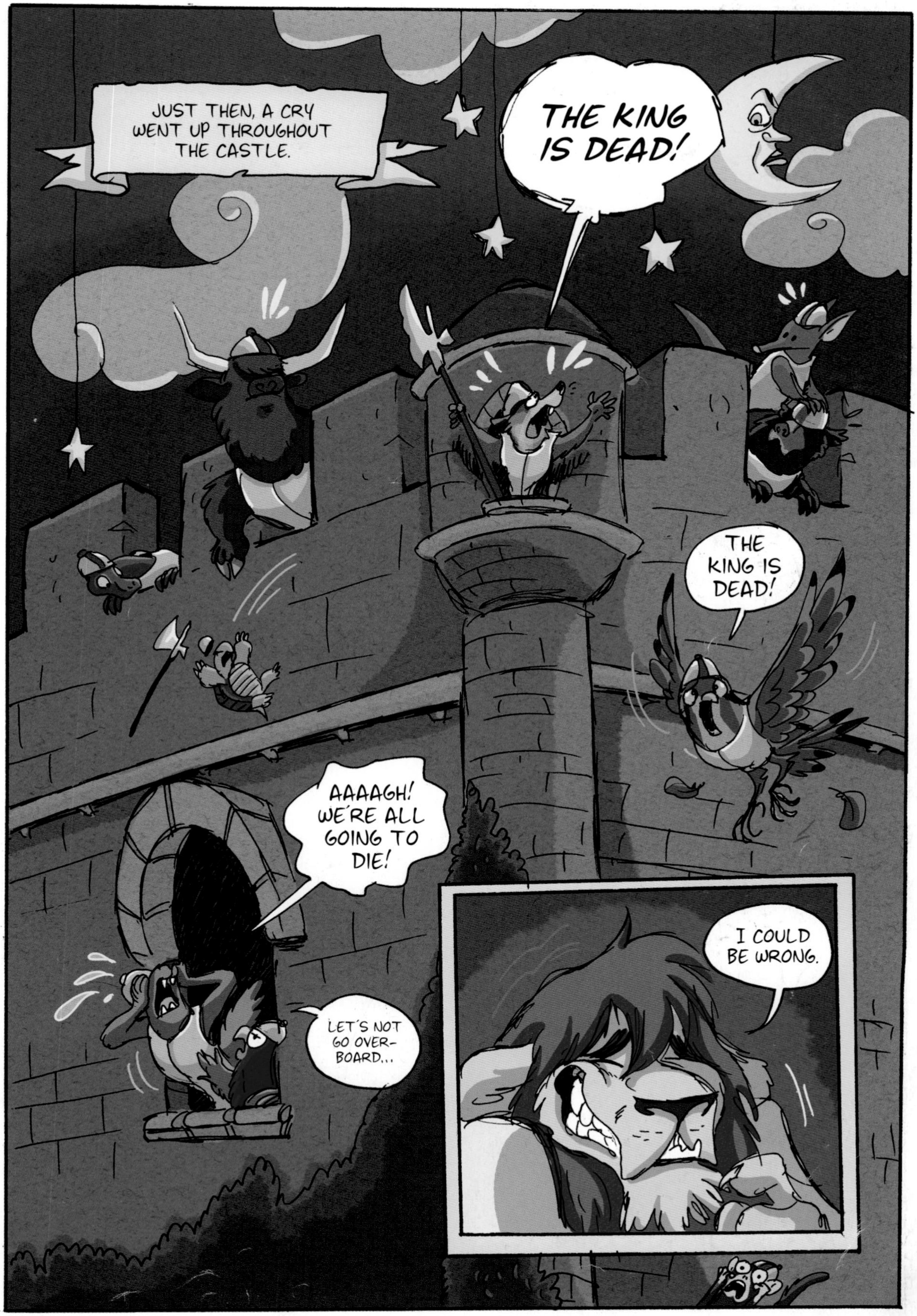
JUST THEN, A CRY WENT UP THROUGHOUT THE CASTLE.
THE KING IS DEAD!
THE KING IS DEAD!
AAAAGH! WE'RE ALL GOING TO DIE!
LET'S NOT GO OVER-BOARD...
I COULD BE WRONG.

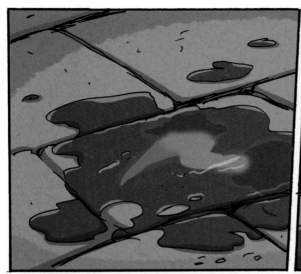

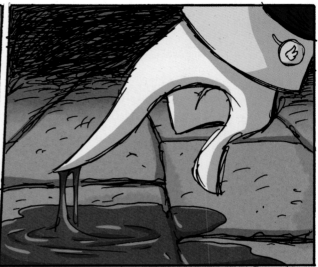

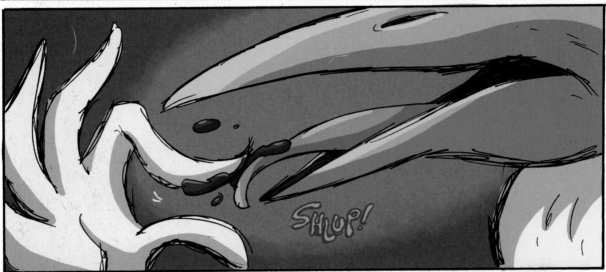

SHLUP!

KETCHUP. NO DOUBT ABOUT IT.

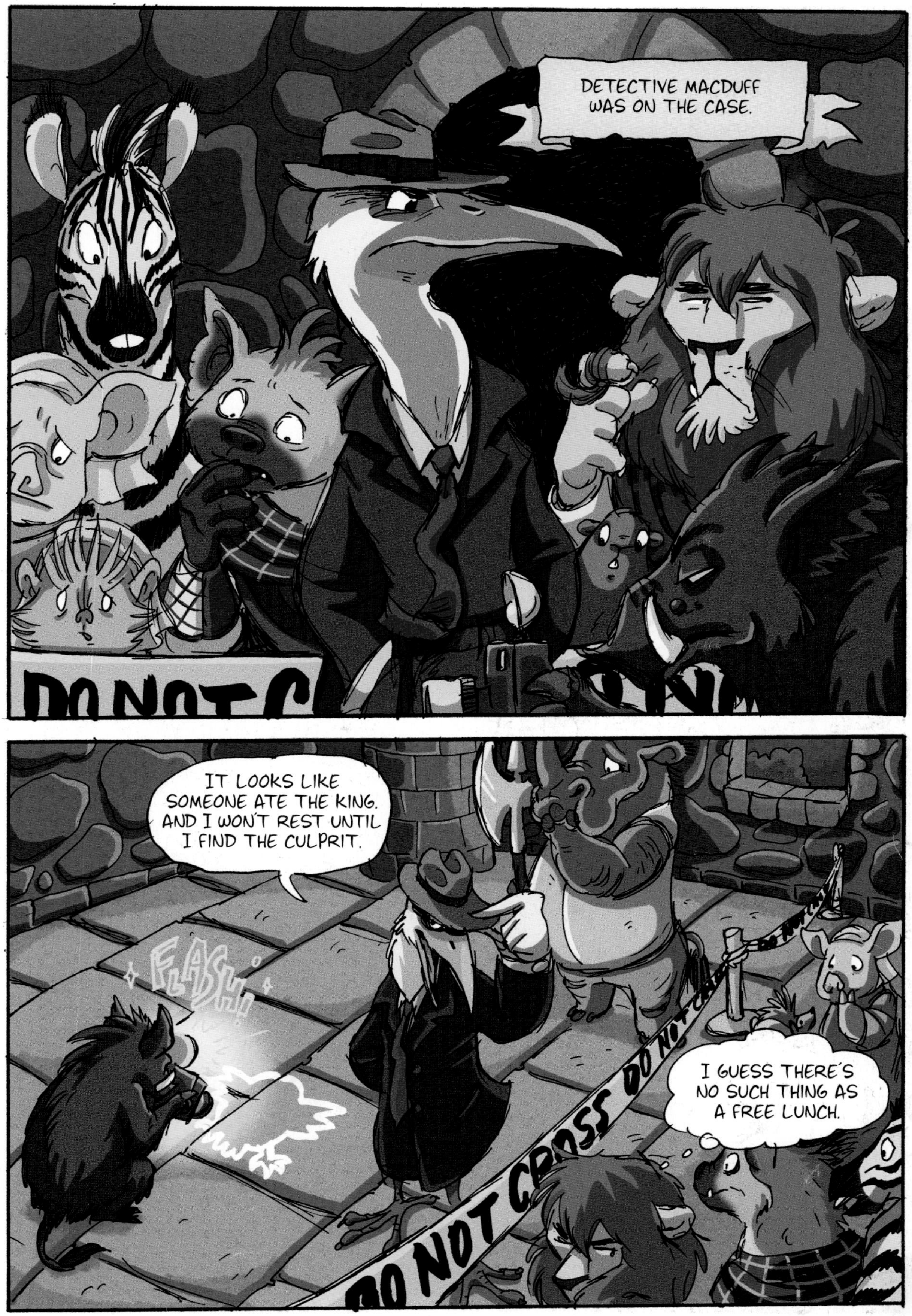
DETECTIVE MACDUFF WAS ON THE CASE.
DO NOT C
IT LOOKS LIKE SOMEONE ATE THE KING. AND I WON'T REST UNTIL I FIND THE CULPRIT.
FLASH!
I GUESS THERE'S NO SUCH THING AS A FREE LUNCH.
DO NOT CROSS DO NOT CROSS
DO NOT CROSS

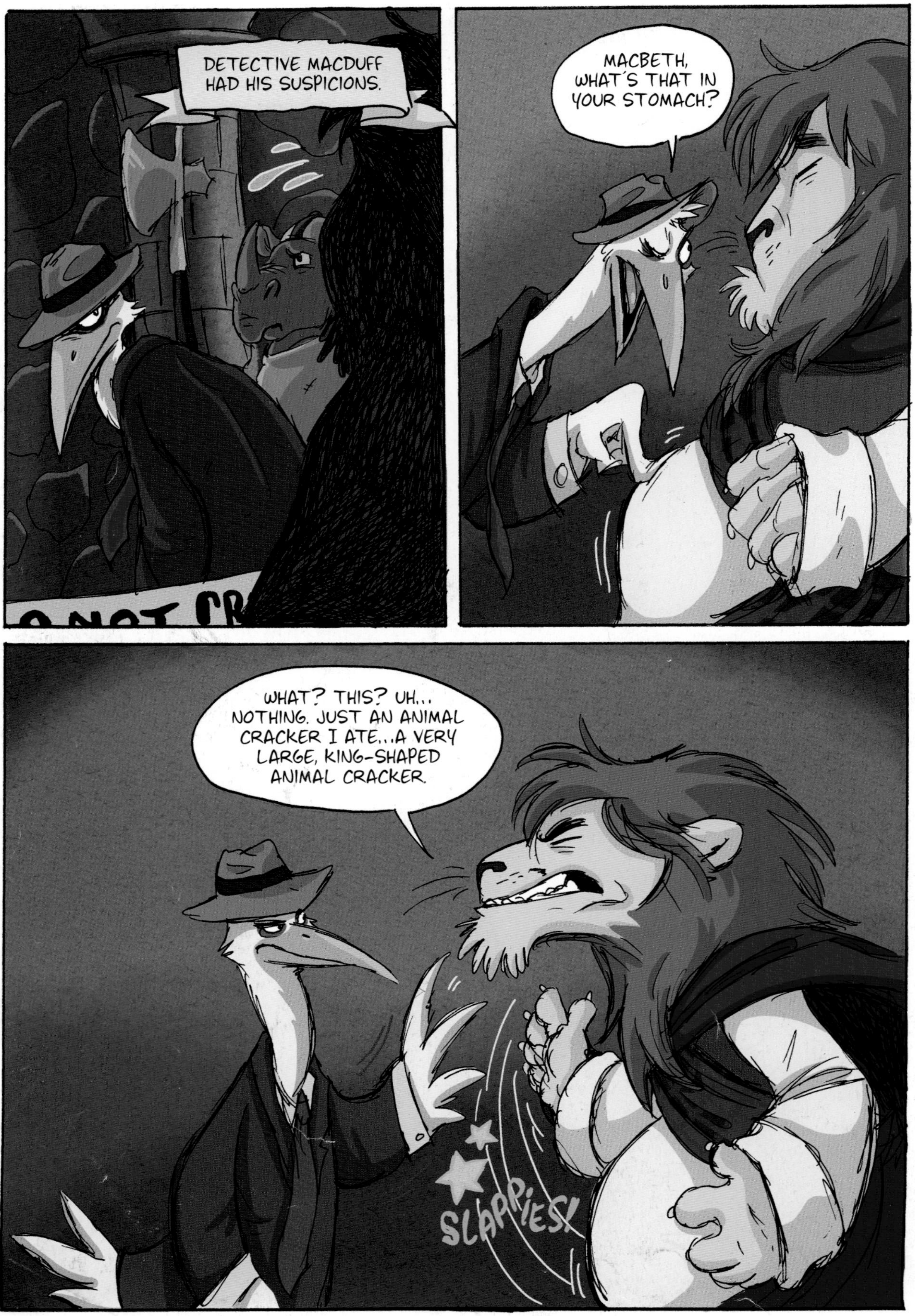
DETECTIVE MACDUFF HAD HIS SUSPICIONS.
MACBETH, WHAT'S THAT IN YOUR STOMACH?
WHAT? THIS? UH... NOTHING. JUST AN ANIMAL CRACKER I ATE...A VERY LARGE, KING-SHAPED ANIMAL CRACKER.
SLAPPIES!

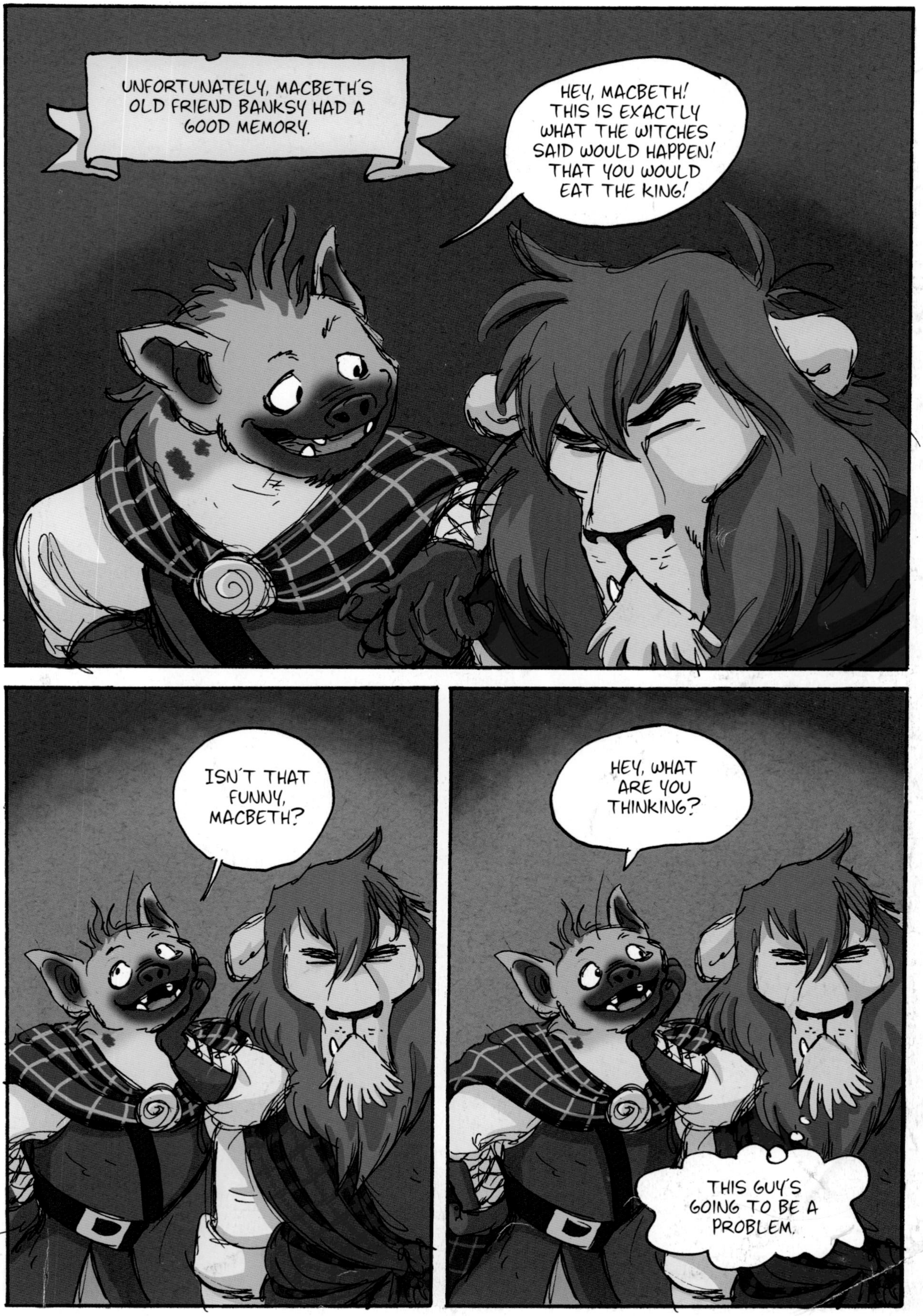
UNFORTUNATELY, MACBETH'S OLD FRIEND BANKSY HAD A GOOD MEMORY.
HEY, MACBETH! THIS IS EXACTLY WHAT THE WITCHES SAID WOULD HAPPEN! THAT YOU WOULD EAT THE KING!
ISN'T THAT FUNNY, MACBETH?
HEY, WHAT ARE YOU THINKING?
THIS GUY'S GOING TO BE A PROBLEM.

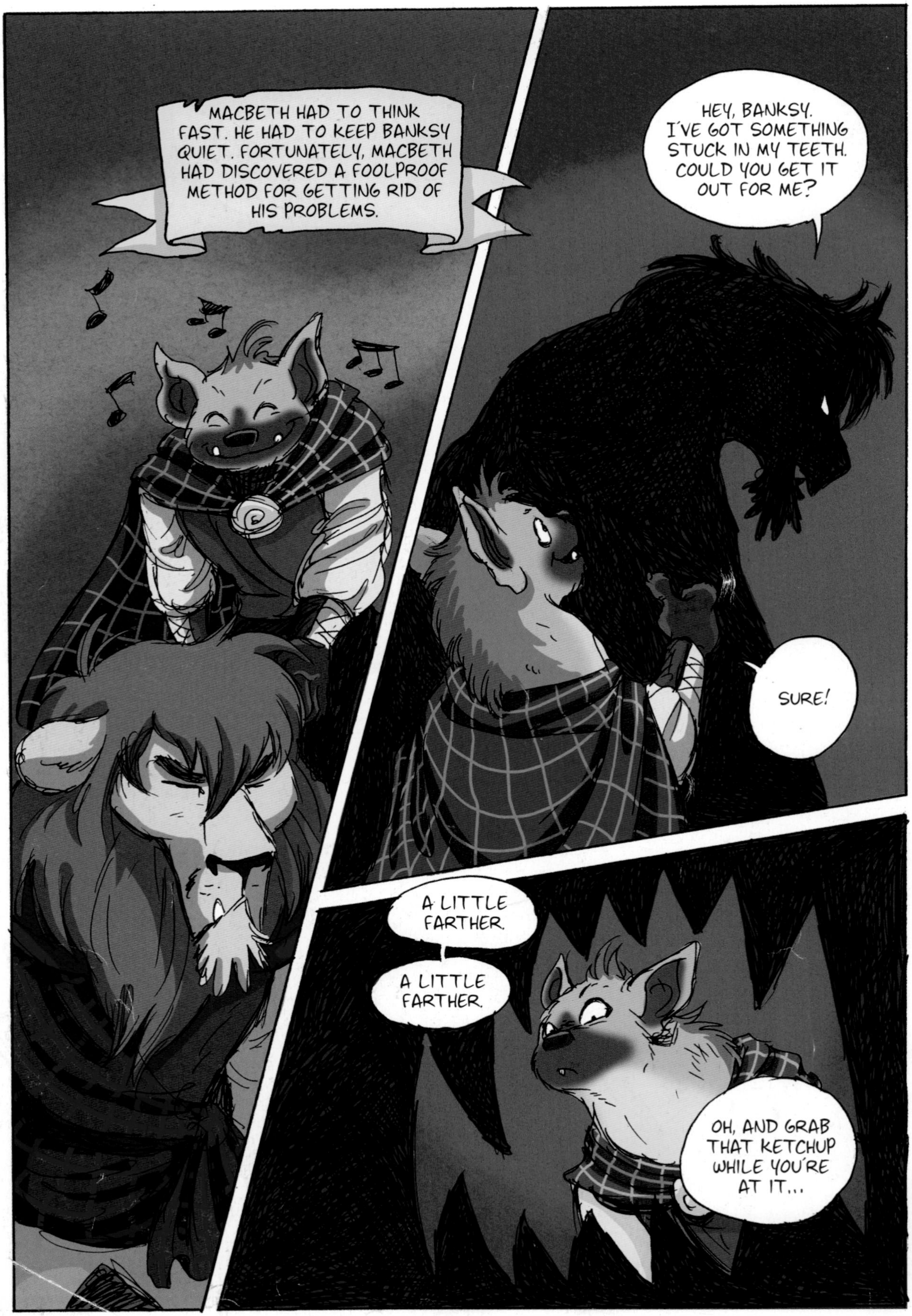
MACBETH HAD TO THINK FAST. HE HAD TO KEEP BANKSY QUIET. FORTUNATELY, MACBETH HAD DISCOVERED A FOOLPROOF METHOD FOR GETTING RID OF HIS PROBLEMS.
HEY, BANKSY. I'VE GOT SOMETHING STUCK IN MY TEETH. COULD YOU GET IT OUT FOR ME?
SURE!
A LITTLE FARTHER.
A LITTLE FARTHER.
OH, AND GRAB THAT KETCHUP WHILE YOU'RE AT IT...

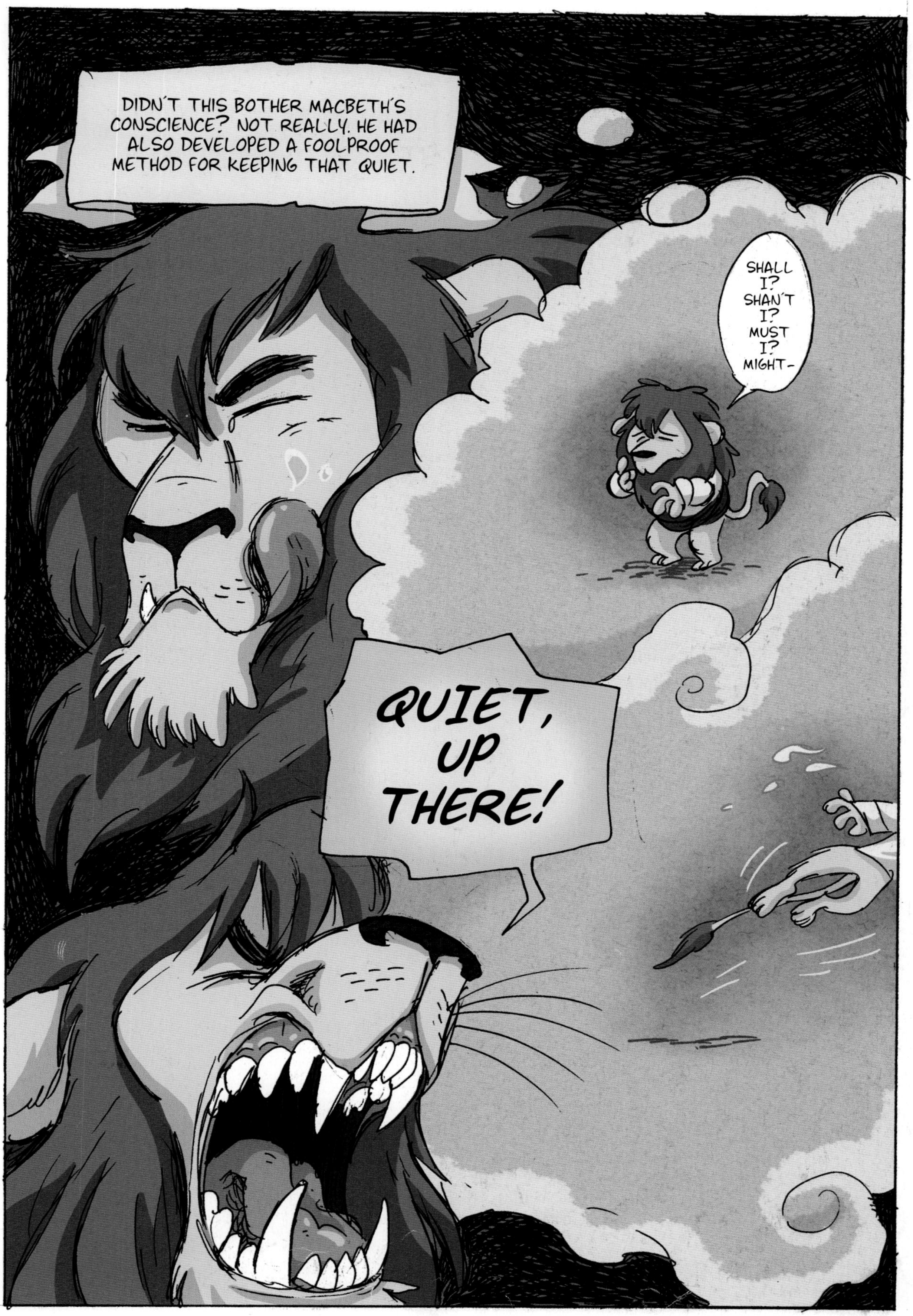

DIDN´T THIS BOTHER MACBETH´S CONSCIENCE? NOT REALLY. HE HAD ALSO DEVELOPED A FOOLPROOF METHOD FOR KEEPING THAT QUIET.
SHALL I? SHAN´T I? MUST I? MIGHT-
QUIET, UP THERE!

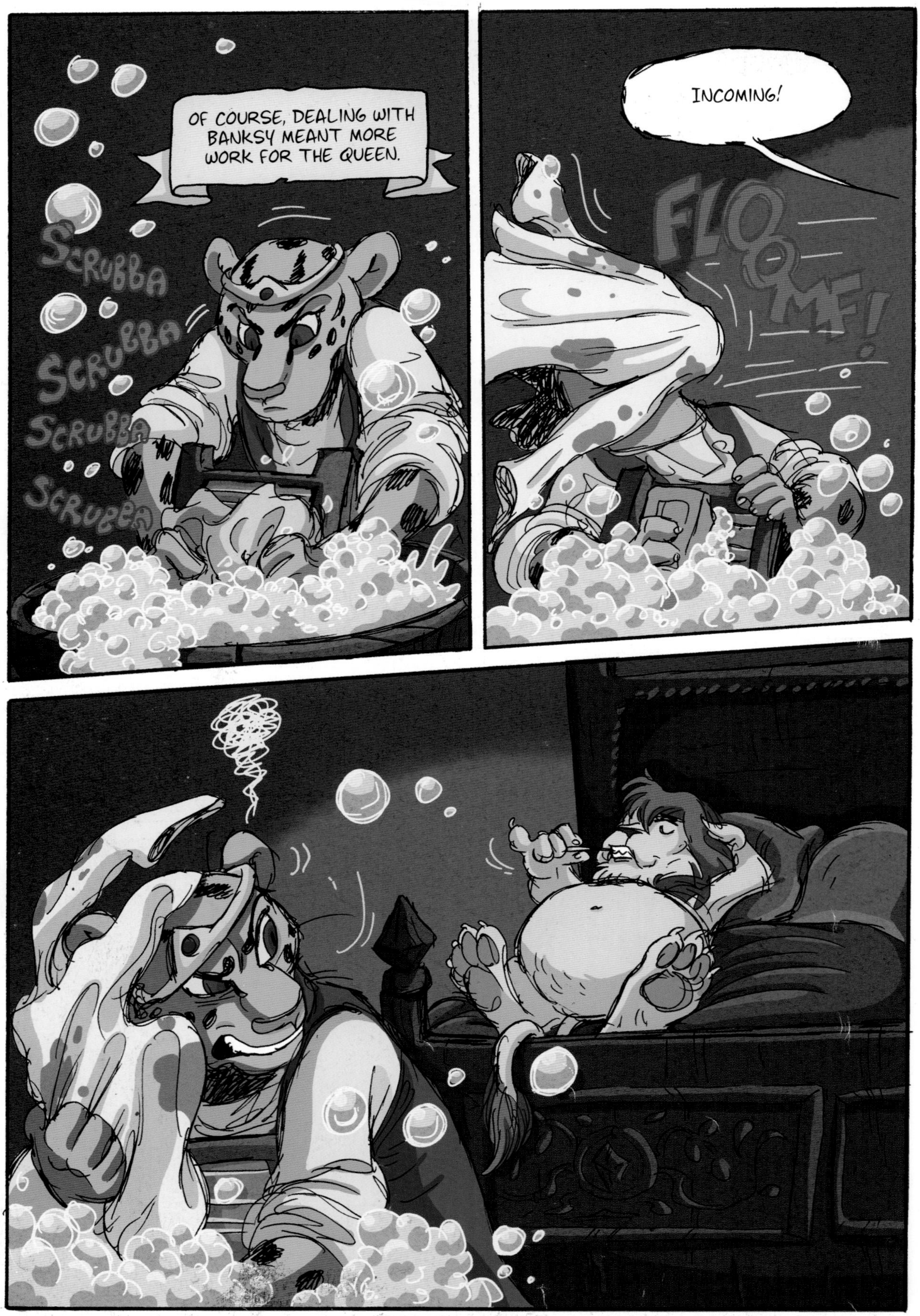
OF COURSE, DEALING WITH BANKSY MEANT MORE WORK FOR THE QUEEN.
SCRUBBA
SCRUBBA
SCRUBBA
SCRUBBA
SCRUBBA
INCOMING!
FLOOMF!

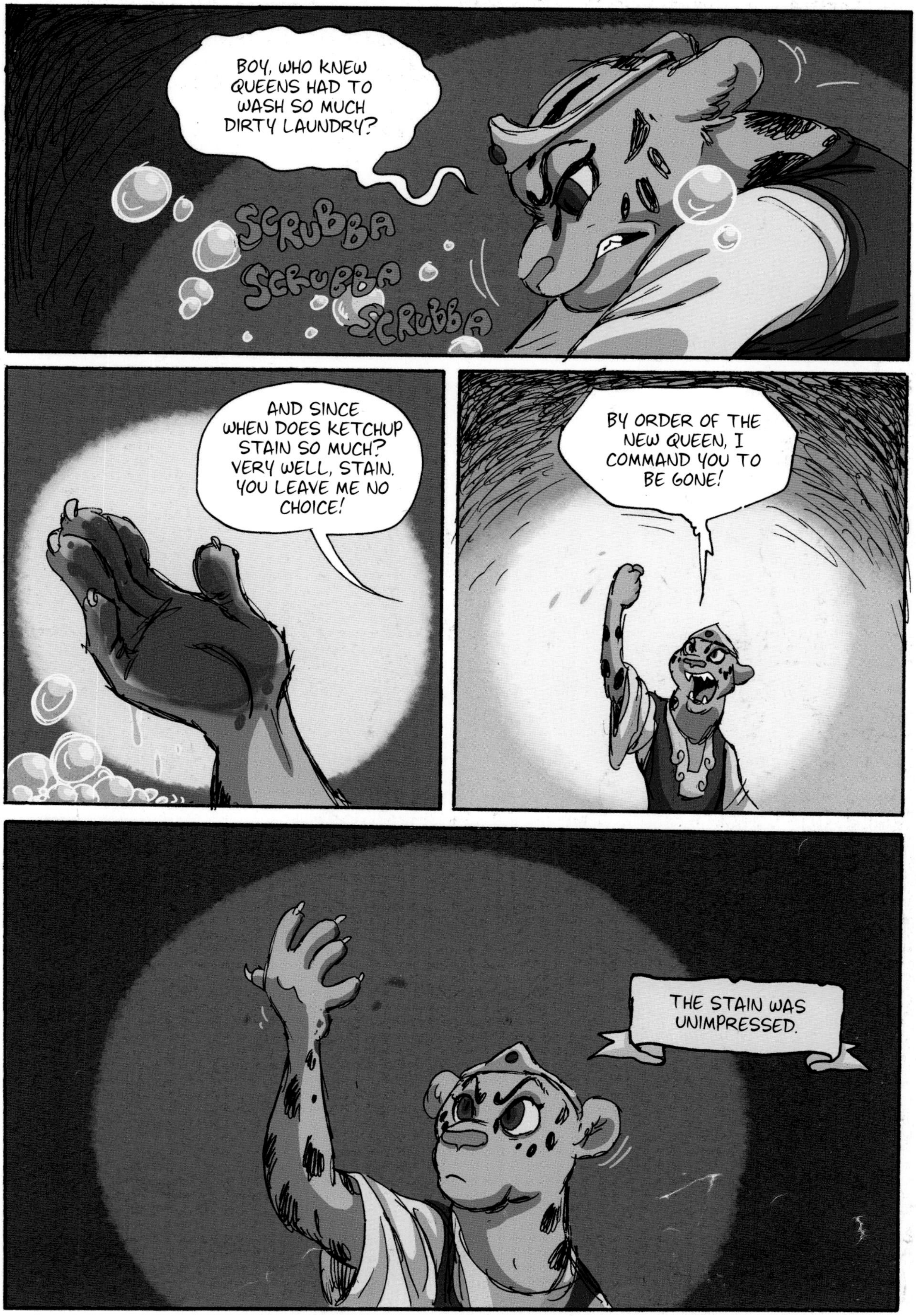
BOY, WHO KNEW QUEENS HAD TO WASH SO MUCH DIRTY LAUNDRY?
SCRUBBA SCRUBBA SCRUBBA
AND SINCE WHEN DOES KETCHUP STAIN SO MUCH? VERY WELL, STAIN. YOU LEAVE ME NO CHOICE!
BY ORDER OF THE NEW QUEEN, I COMMAND YOU TO BE GONE!
THE STAIN WAS UNIMPRESSED.

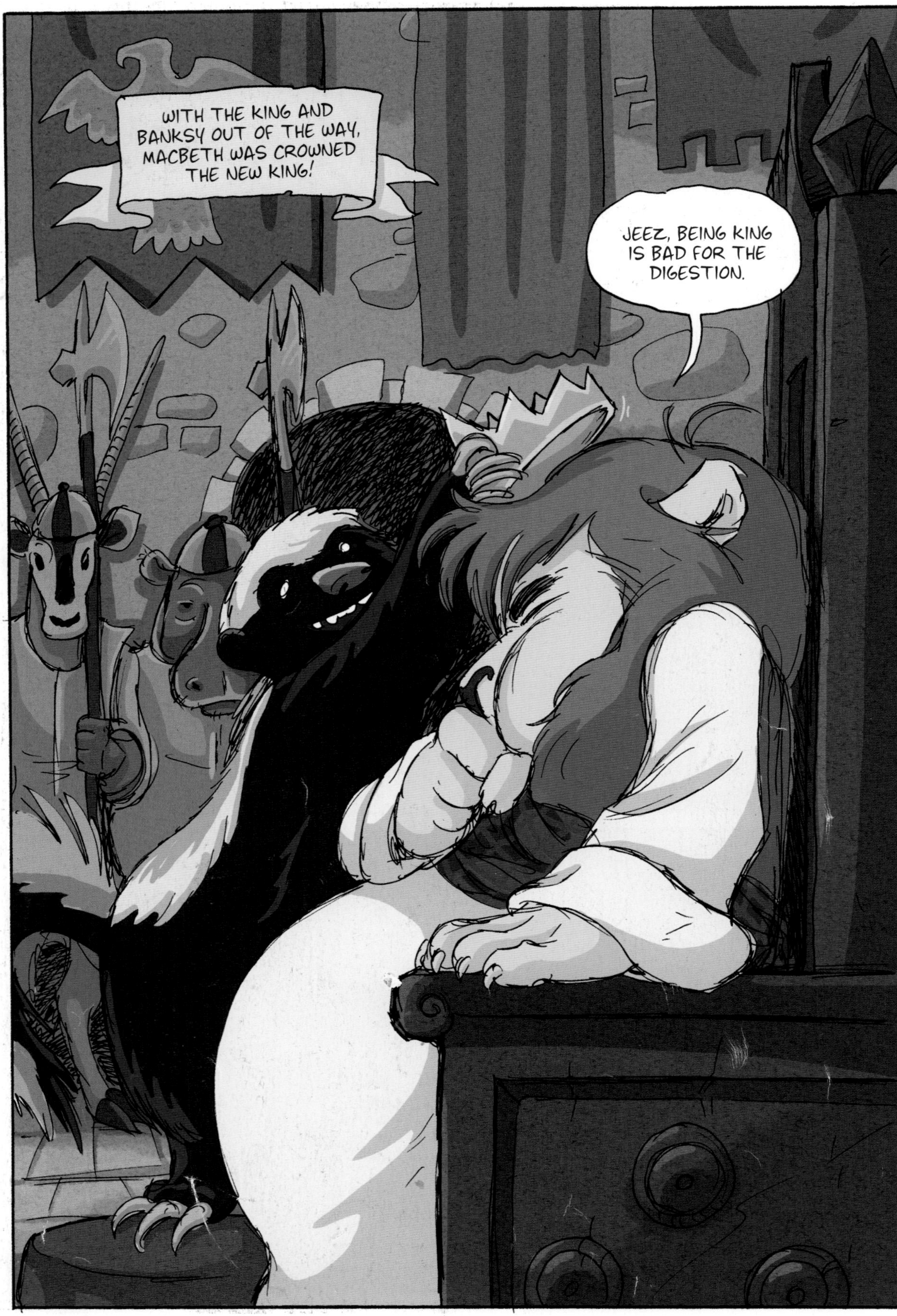
WITH THE KING AND BANKSY OUT OF THE WAY, MACBETH WAS CROWNED THE NEW KING!
JEEZ, BEING KING IS BAD FOR THE DIGESTION.

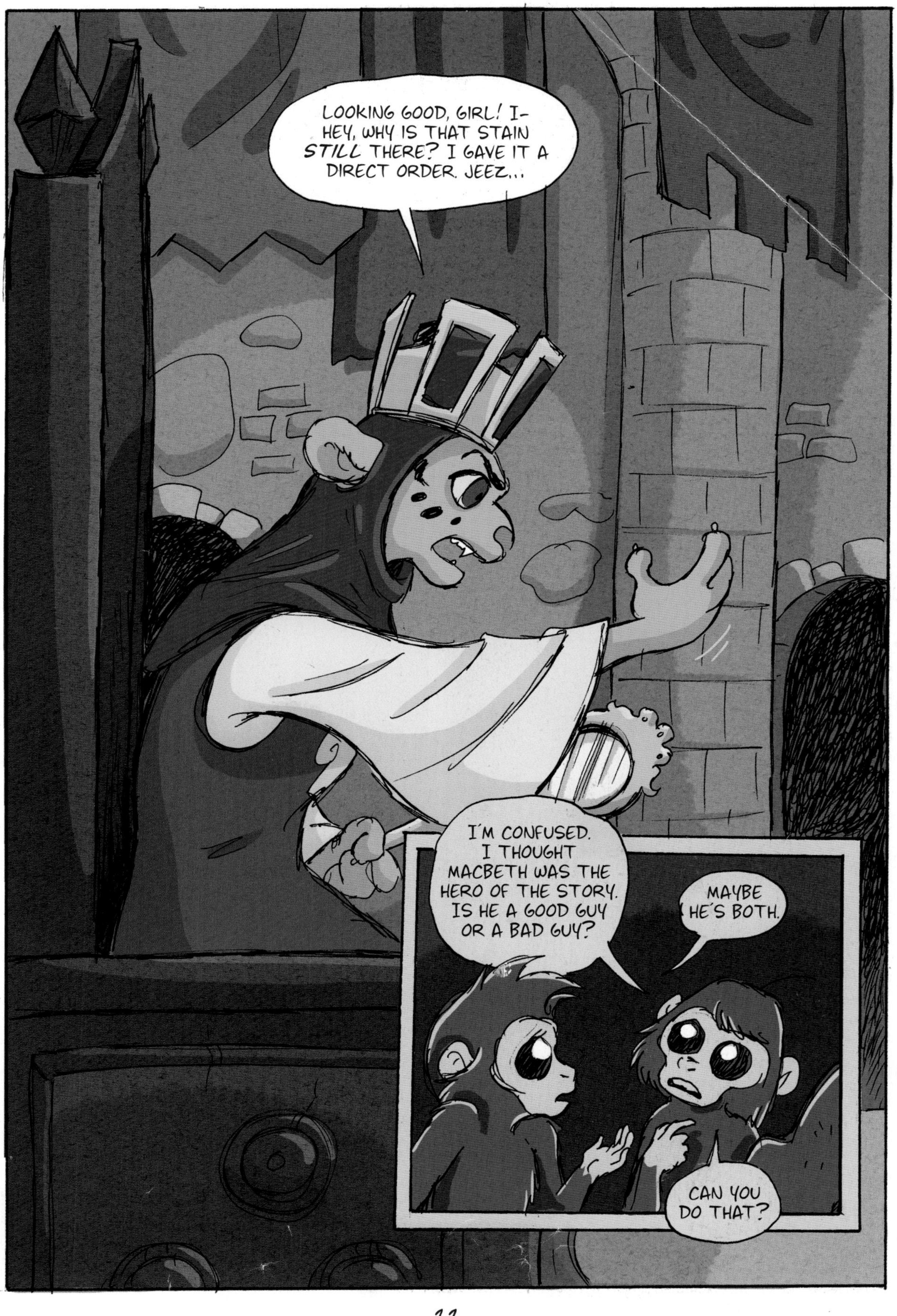
LOOKING GOOD, GIRL! I- HEY, WHY IS THAT STAIN *STILL* THERE? I GAVE IT A DIRECT ORDER. JEEZ...
I'M CONFUSED. I THOUGHT MACBETH WAS THE HERO OF THE STORY. IS HE A GOOD GUY OR A BAD GUY?
MAYBE HE'S BOTH.
CAN YOU DO THAT?

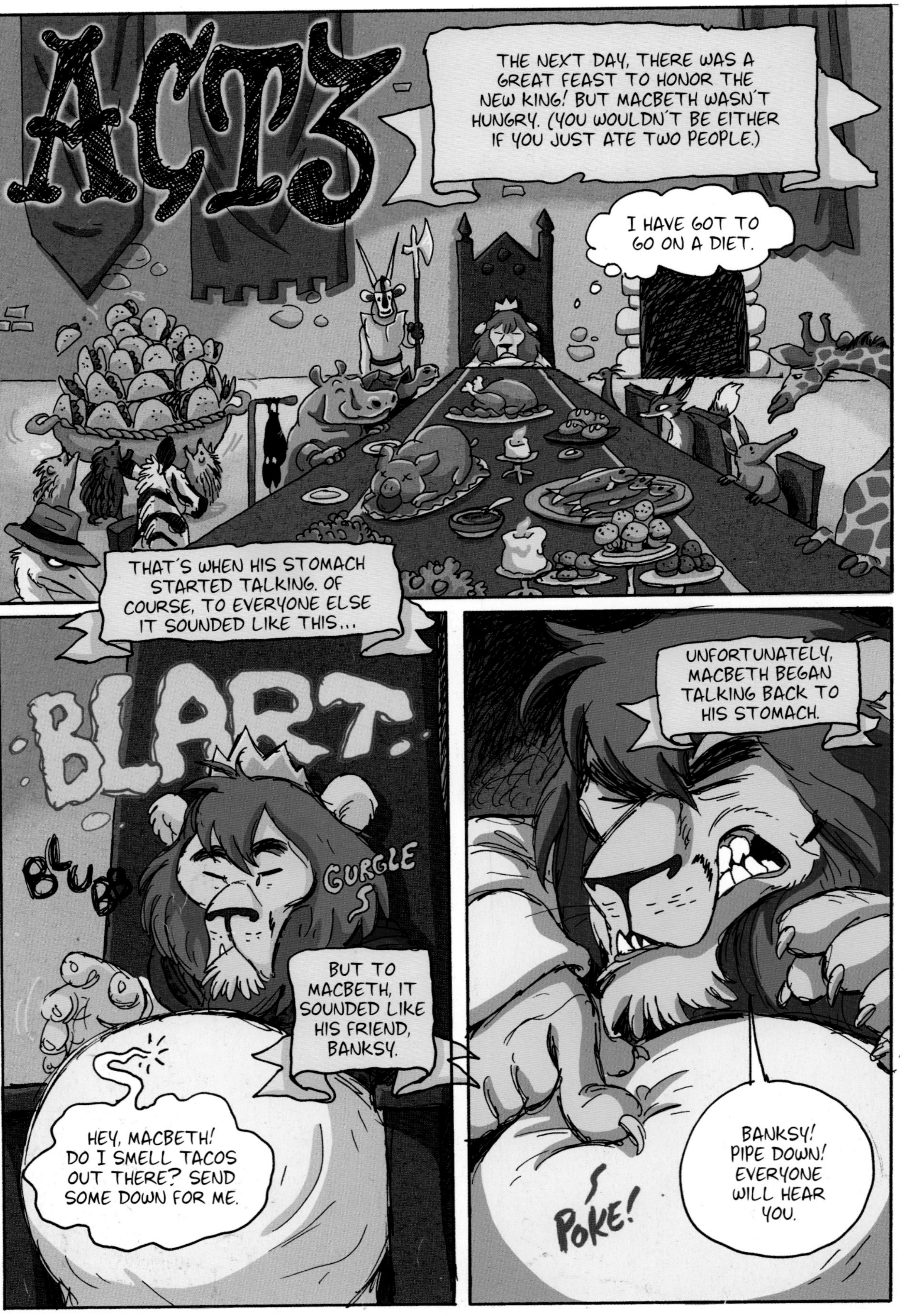

ACT 3
THE NEXT DAY, THERE WAS A GREAT FEAST TO HONOR THE NEW KING! BUT MACBETH WASN'T HUNGRY. (YOU WOULDN'T BE EITHER IF YOU JUST ATE TWO PEOPLE.)
I HAVE GOT TO GO ON A DIET.
THAT'S WHEN HIS STOMACH STARTED TALKING. OF COURSE, TO EVERYONE ELSE IT SOUNDED LIKE THIS...
BLART
BLUBB
GURGLE
BUT TO MACBETH, IT SOUNDED LIKE HIS FRIEND, BANKSY.
HEY, MACBETH! DO I SMELL TACOS OUT THERE? SEND SOME DOWN FOR ME.
UNFORTUNATELY, MACBETH BEGAN TALKING BACK TO HIS STOMACH.
POKE!
BANKSY! PIPE DOWN! EVERYONE WILL HEAR YOU.

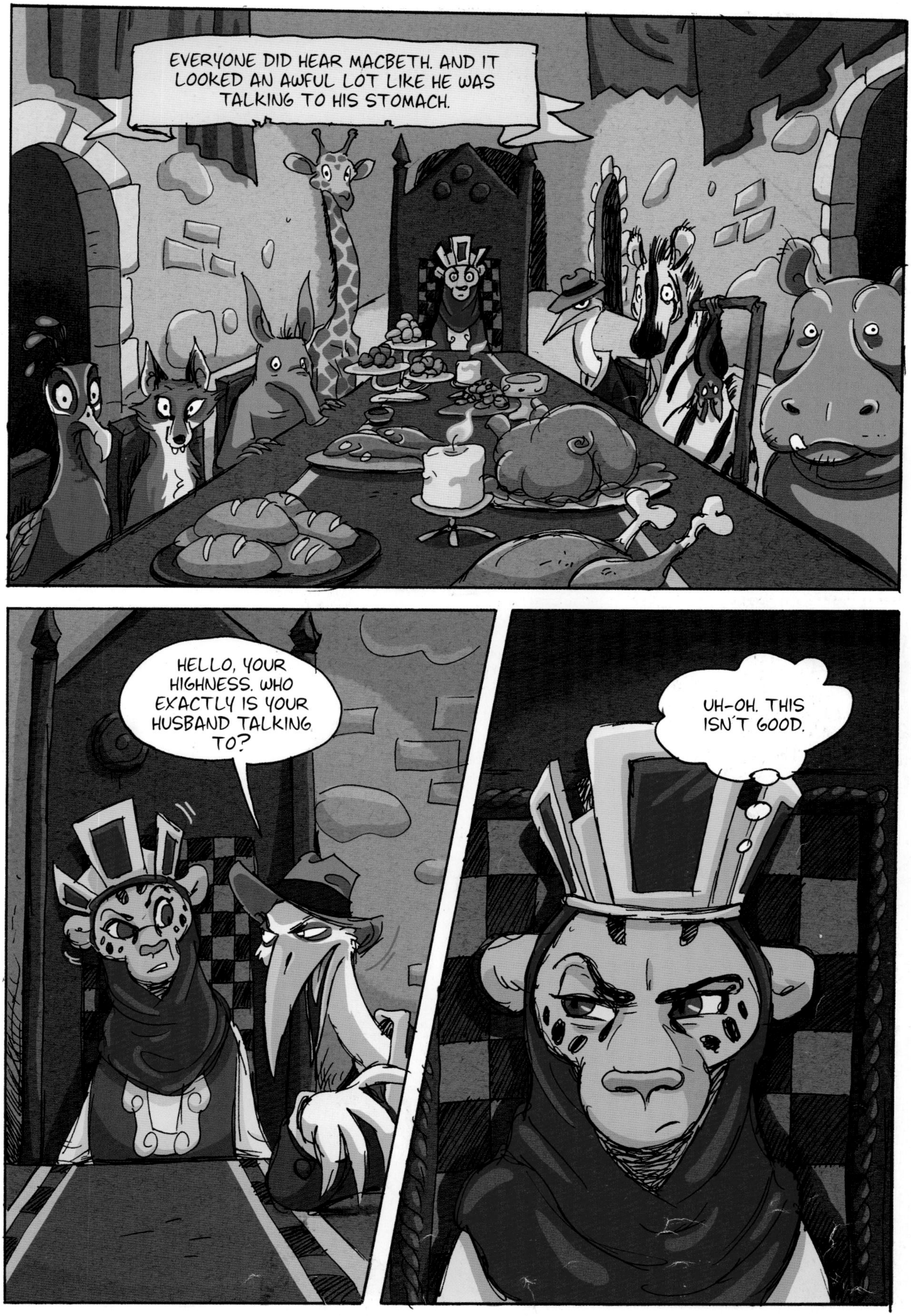
EVERYONE DID HEAR MACBETH. AND IT LOOKED AN AWFUL LOT LIKE HE WAS TALKING TO HIS STOMACH.
HELLO, YOUR HIGHNESS. WHO EXACTLY IS YOUR HUSBAND TALKING TO?
UH-OH. THIS ISN'T GOOD.

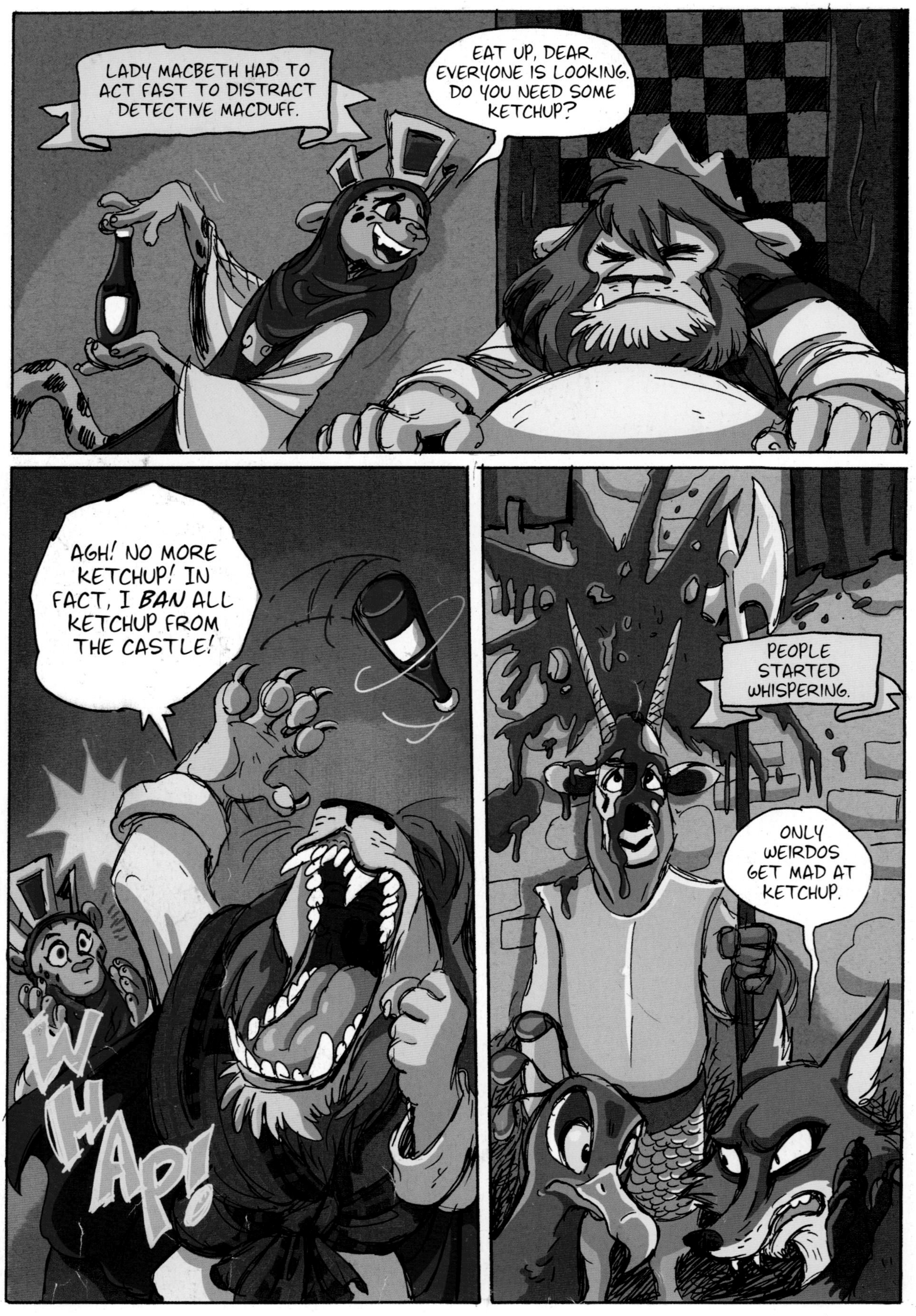
LADY MACBETH HAD TO ACT FAST TO DISTRACT DETECTIVE MACDUFF.
EAT UP, DEAR. EVERYONE IS LOOKING. DO YOU NEED SOME KETCHUP?
AGH! NO MORE KETCHUP! IN FACT, I BAN ALL KETCHUP FROM THE CASTLE!
WHAP!
PEOPLE STARTED WHISPERING.
ONLY WEIRDOS GET MAD AT KETCHUP.

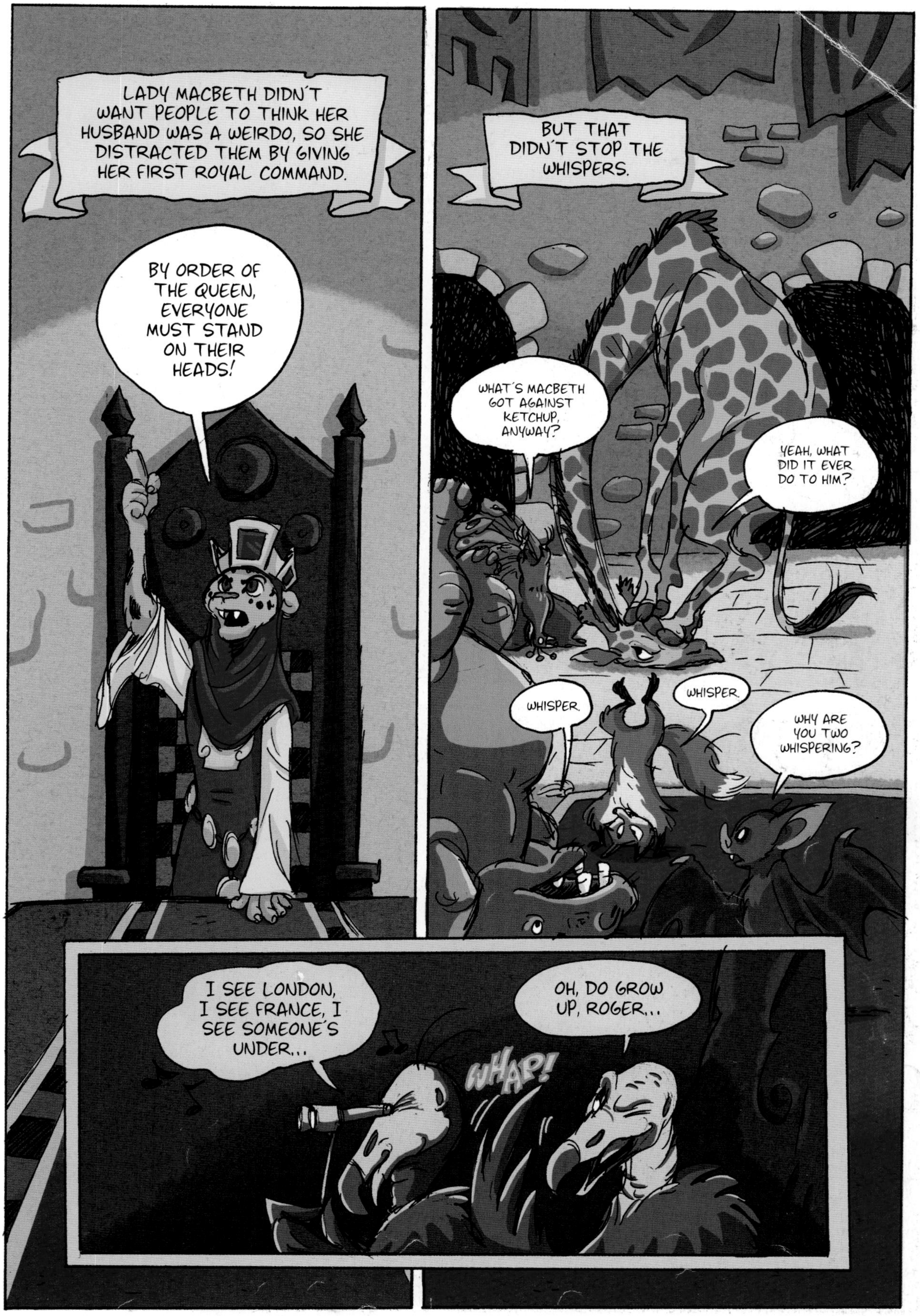
LADY MACBETH DIDN'T WANT PEOPLE TO THINK HER HUSBAND WAS A WEIRDO, SO SHE DISTRACTED THEM BY GIVING HER FIRST ROYAL COMMAND.
BY ORDER OF THE QUEEN, EVERYONE MUST STAND ON THEIR HEADS!
BUT THAT DIDN'T STOP THE WHISPERS.
WHAT'S MACBETH GOT AGAINST KETCHUP, ANYWAY?
YEAH, WHAT DID IT EVER DO TO HIM?
WHISPER.
WHISPER.
WHY ARE YOU TWO WHISPERING?
I SEE LONDON, I SEE FRANCE, I SEE SOMEONE'S UNDER...
WHAP!
OH, DO GROW UP, ROGER...

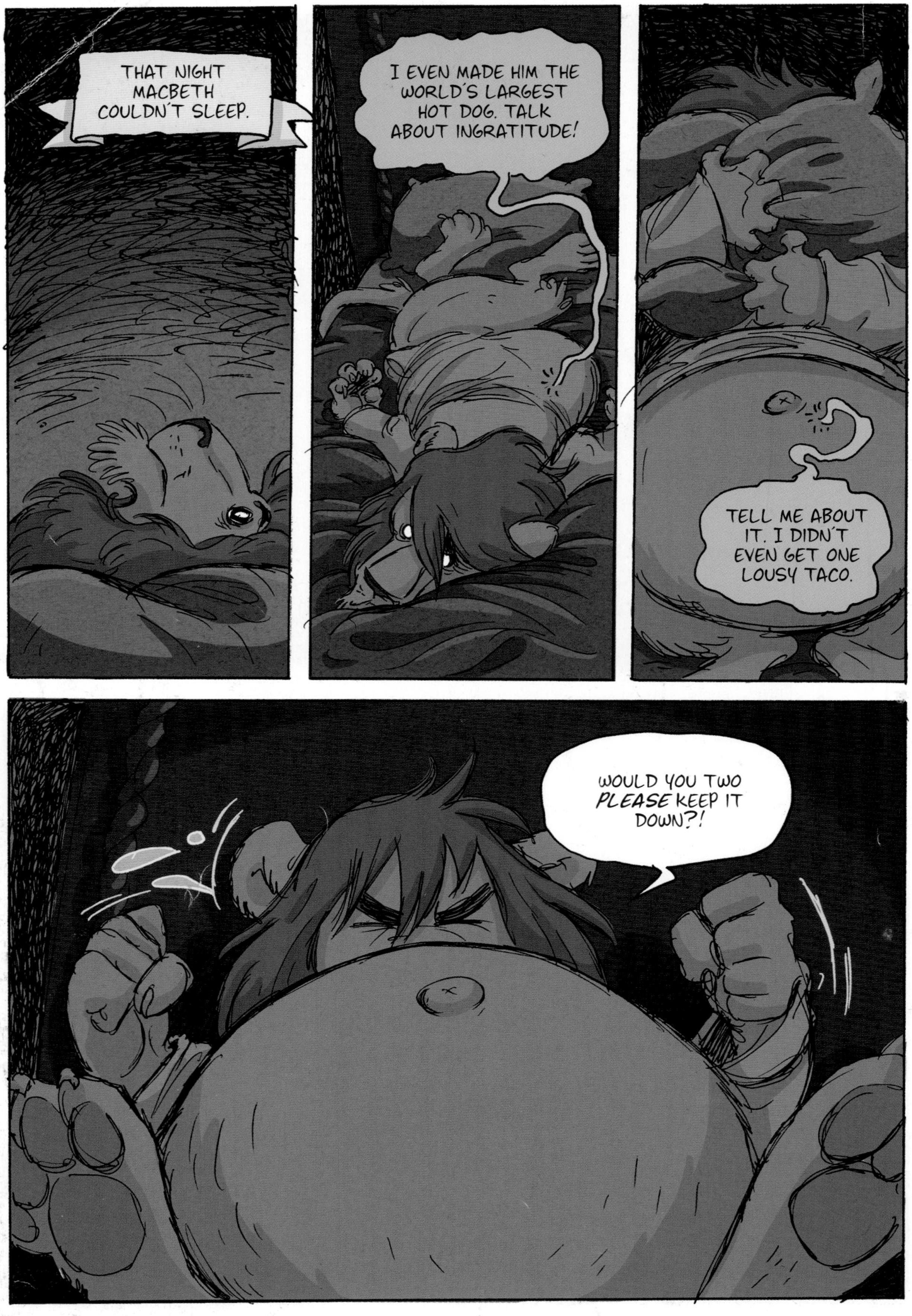
THAT NIGHT MACBETH COULDN'T SLEEP.
I EVEN MADE HIM THE WORLD'S LARGEST HOT DOG. TALK ABOUT INGRATITUDE!
TELL ME ABOUT IT. I DIDN'T EVEN GET ONE LOUSY TACO.
WOULD YOU TWO *PLEASE* KEEP IT DOWN?!

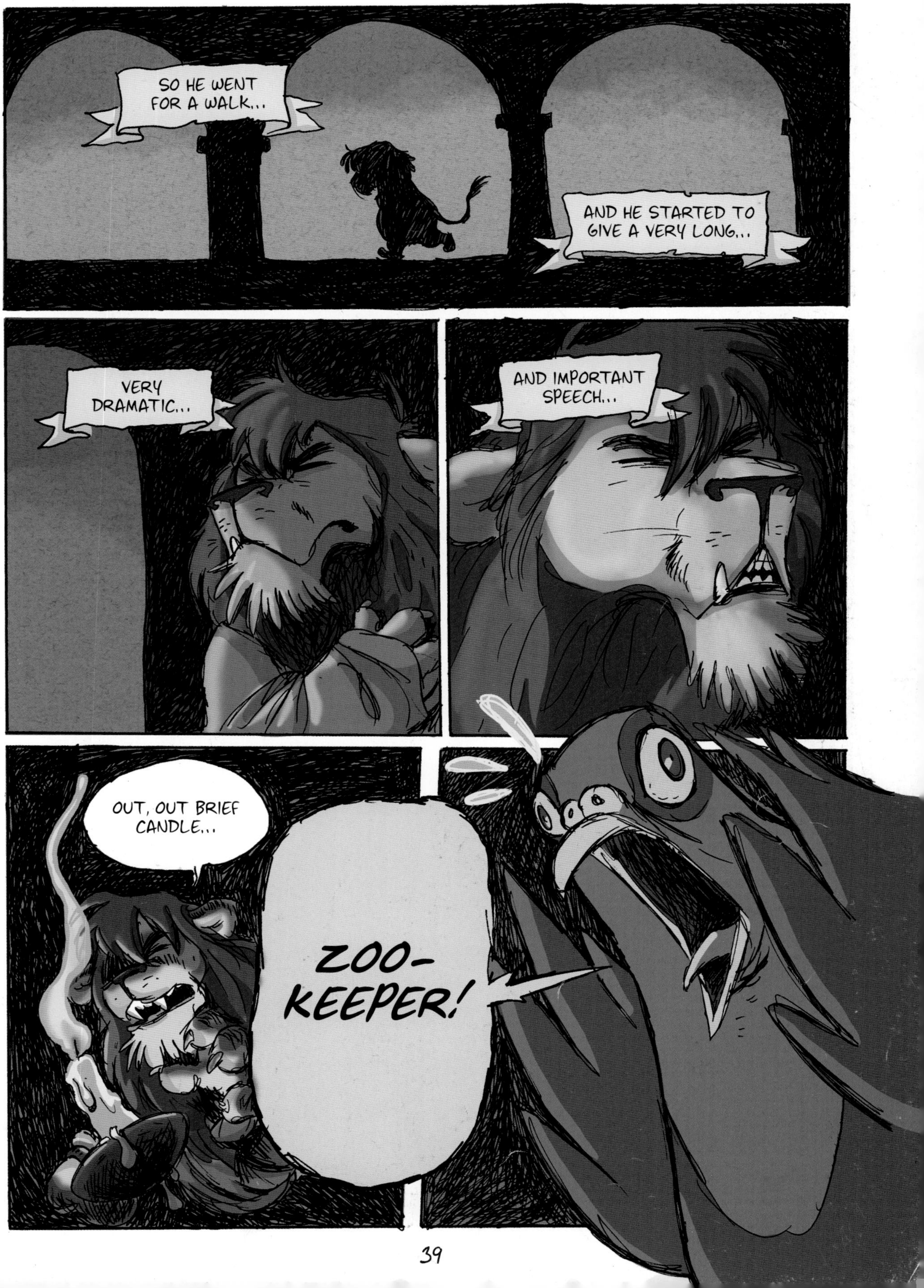
SO HE WENT FOR A WALK...
AND HE STARTED TO GIVE A VERY LONG...
VERY DRAMATIC...
AND IMPORTANT SPEECH...
OUT, OUT BRIEF CANDLE...
ZOO-KEEPER!

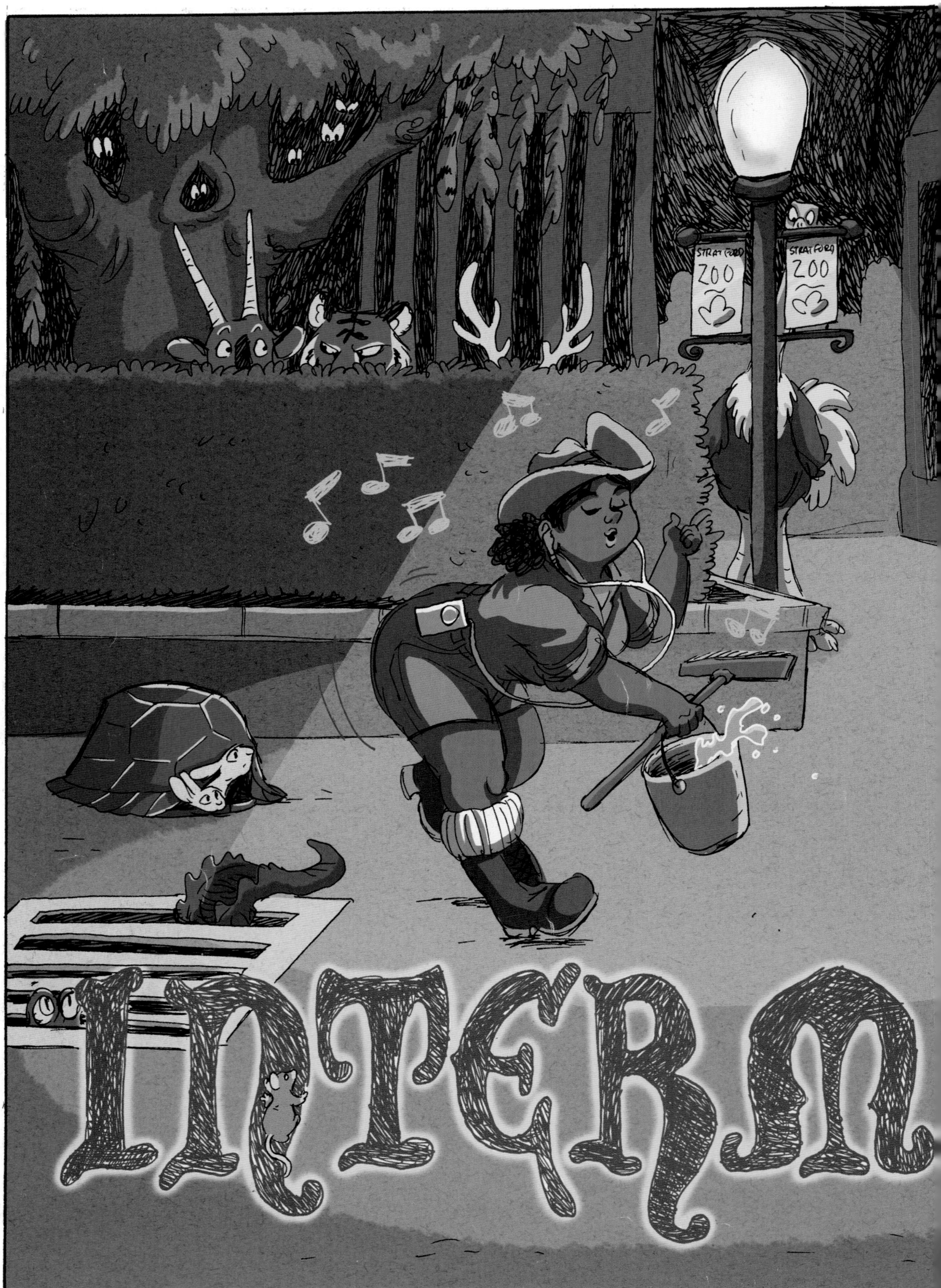
STRATFORD
ZOO
STRATFORD
ZOO
INTERN

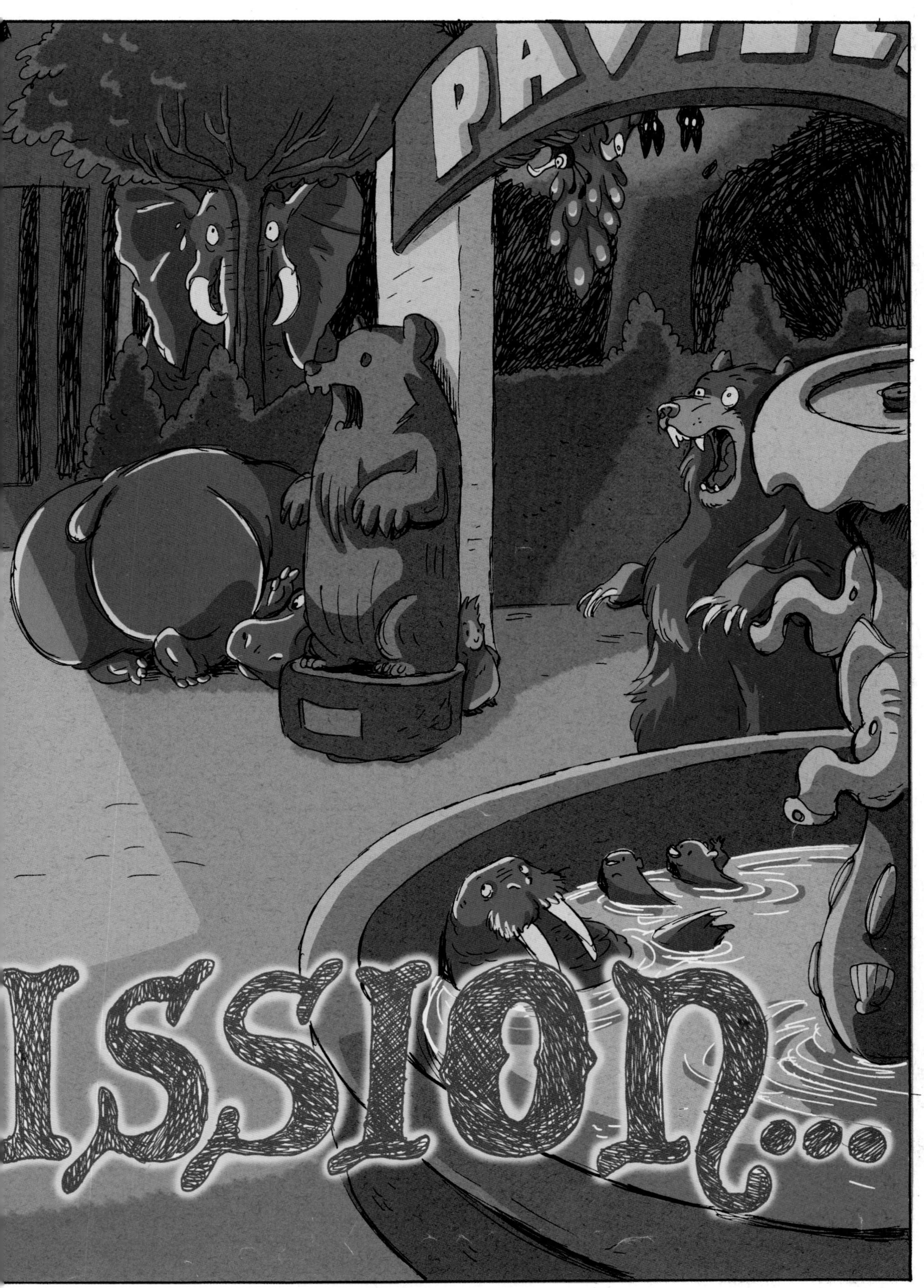
PAV
ission...

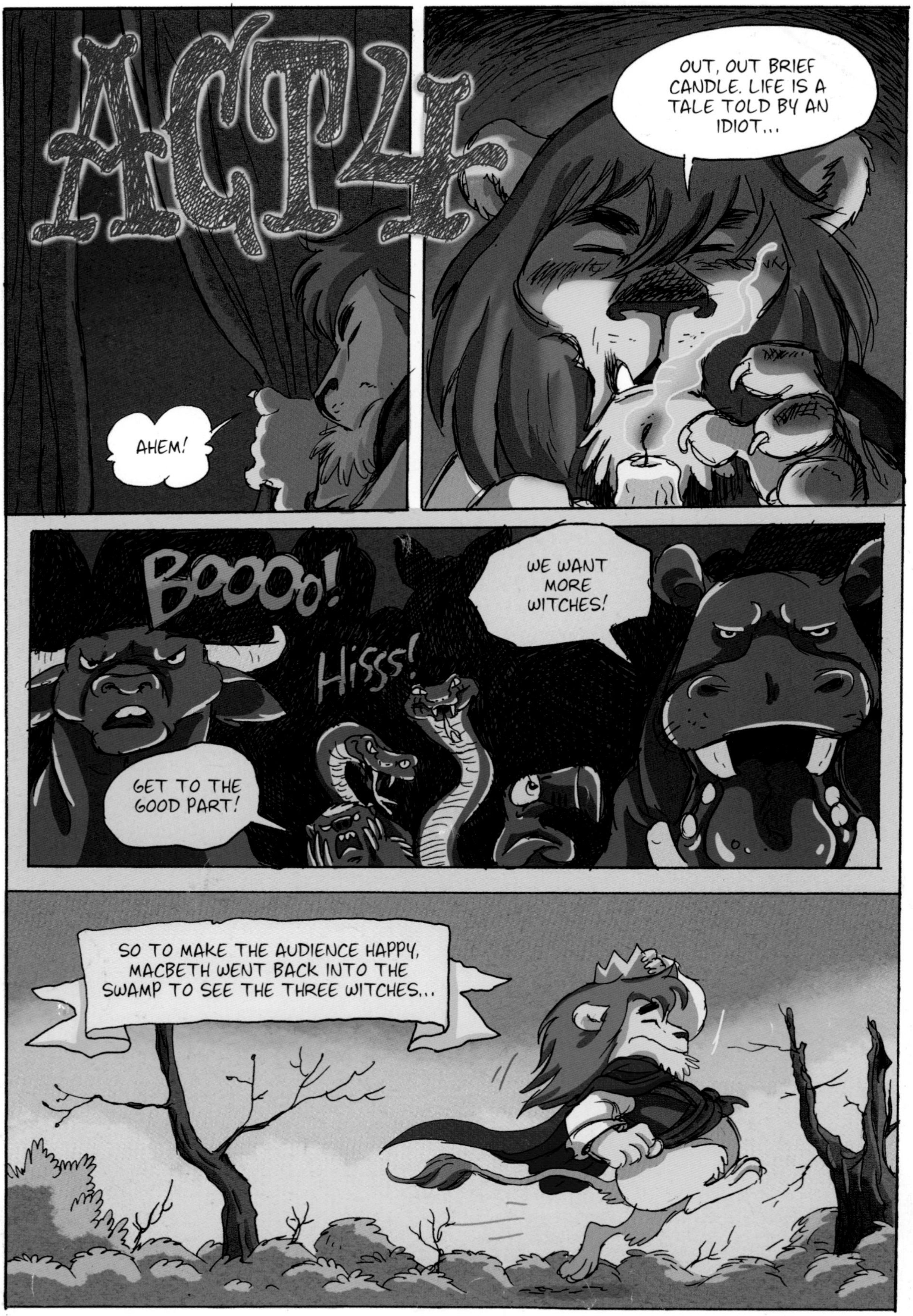
ACT 4
AHEM!
OUT, OUT BRIEF CANDLE. LIFE IS A TALE TOLD BY AN IDIOT...
BOOOOO!
HISSS!
WE WANT MORE WITCHES!
GET TO THE GOOD PART!
SO TO MAKE THE AUDIENCE HAPPY, MACBETH WENT BACK INTO THE SWAMP TO SEE THE THREE WITCHES...

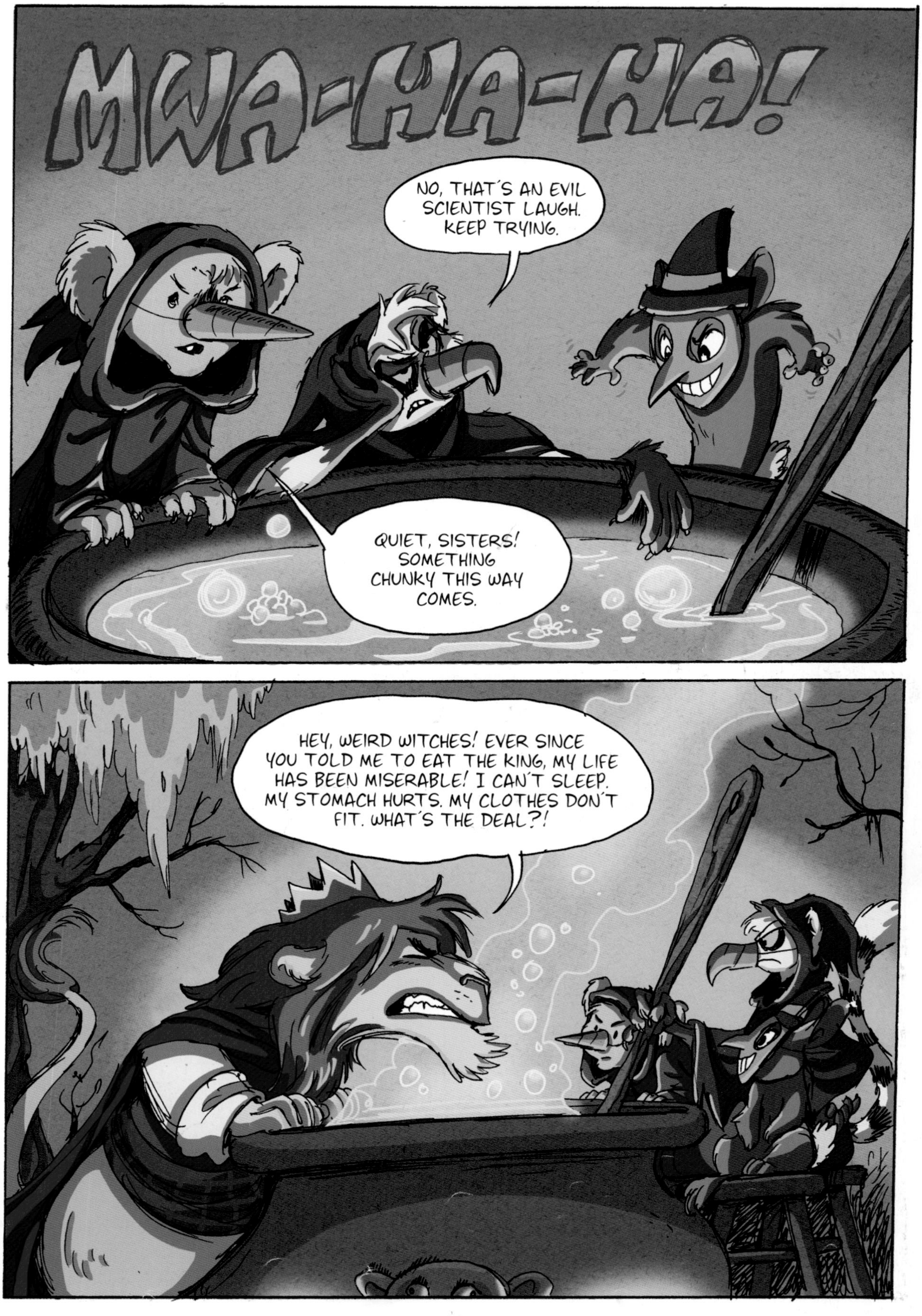
MWA-HA-HA!
NO, THAT´S AN EVIL SCIENTIST LAUGH. KEEP TRYING.
QUIET, SISTERS! SOMETHING CHUNKY THIS WAY COMES.
HEY, WEIRD WITCHES! EVER SINCE YOU TOLD ME TO EAT THE KING, MY LIFE HAS BEEN MISERABLE! I CAN´T SLEEP. MY STOMACH HURTS. MY CLOTHES DON´T FIT. WHAT´S THE DEAL?!

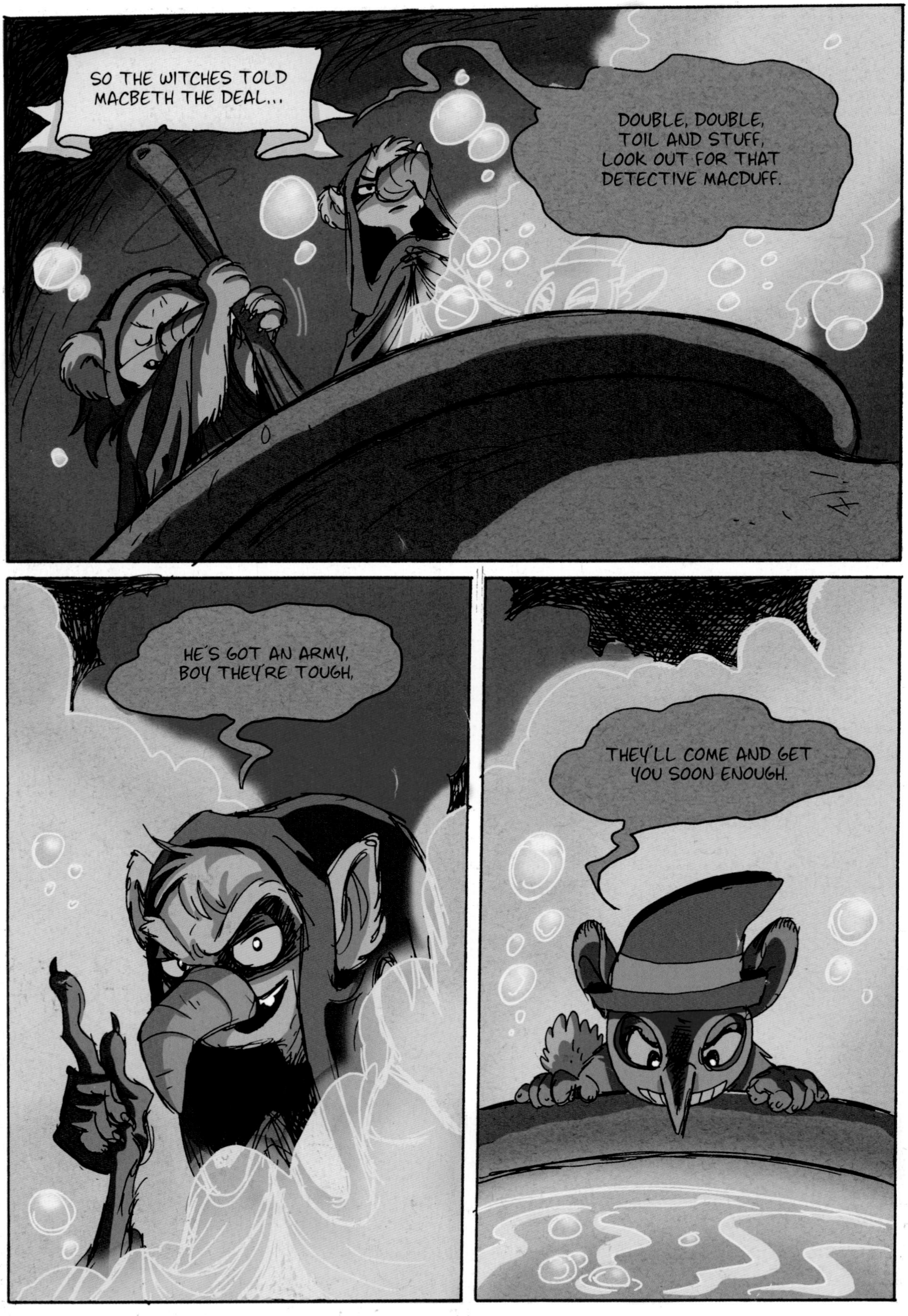

SO THE WITCHES TOLD MACBETH THE DEAL...
DOUBLE, DOUBLE, TOIL AND STUFF, LOOK OUT FOR THAT DETECTIVE MACDUFF.
HE'S GOT AN ARMY, BOY THEY'RE TOUGH,
THEY'LL COME AND GET YOU SOON ENOUGH.

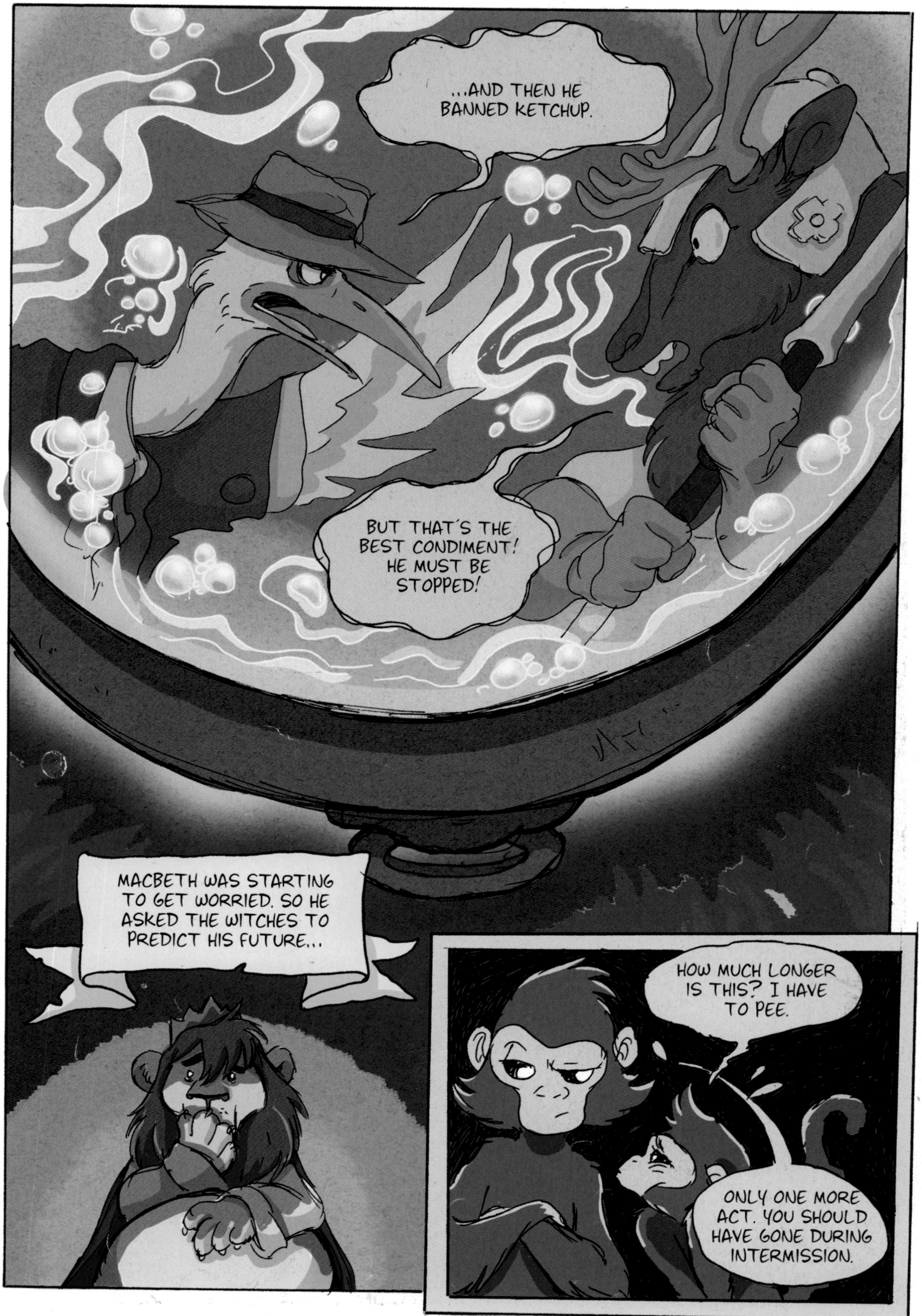
...AND THEN HE BANNED KETCHUP.
BUT THAT'S THE BEST CONDIMENT! HE MUST BE STOPPED!
MACBETH WAS STARTING TO GET WORRIED. SO HE ASKED THE WITCHES TO PREDICT HIS FUTURE...
HOW MUCH LONGER IS THIS? I HAVE TO PEE.
ONLY ONE MORE ACT. YOU SHOULD HAVE GONE DURING INTERMISSION.

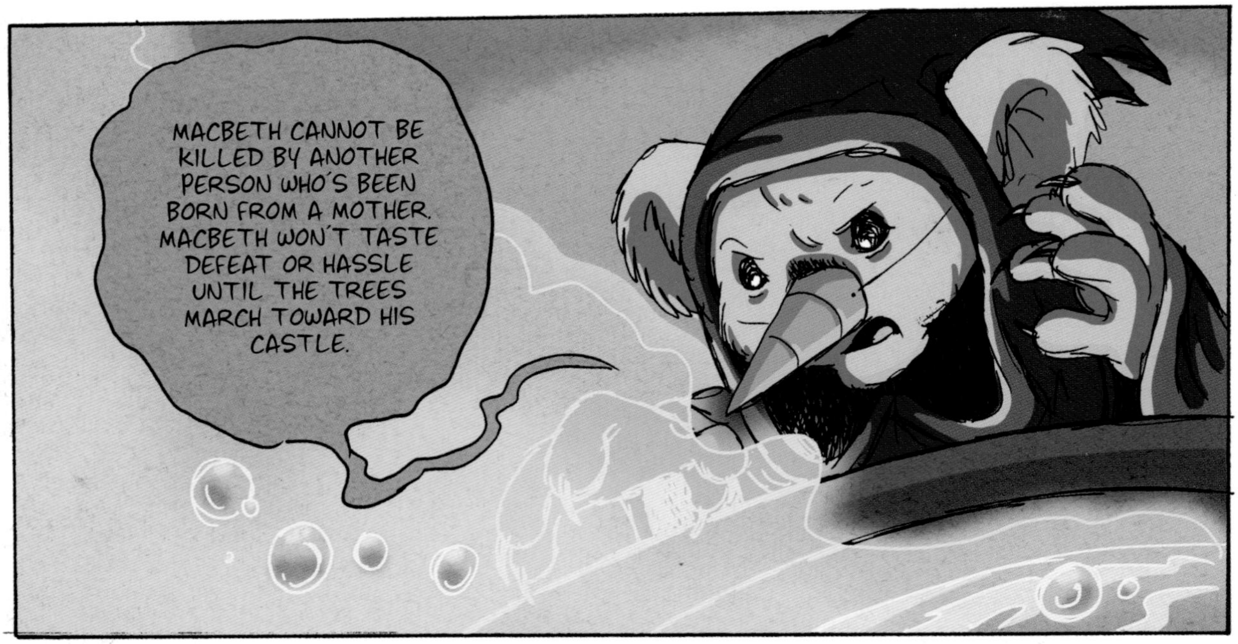
MACBETH CANNOT BE KILLED BY ANOTHER PERSON WHO'S BEEN BORN FROM A MOTHER. MACBETH WON'T TASTE DEFEAT OR HASSLE UNTIL THE TREES MARCH TOWARD HIS CASTLE.

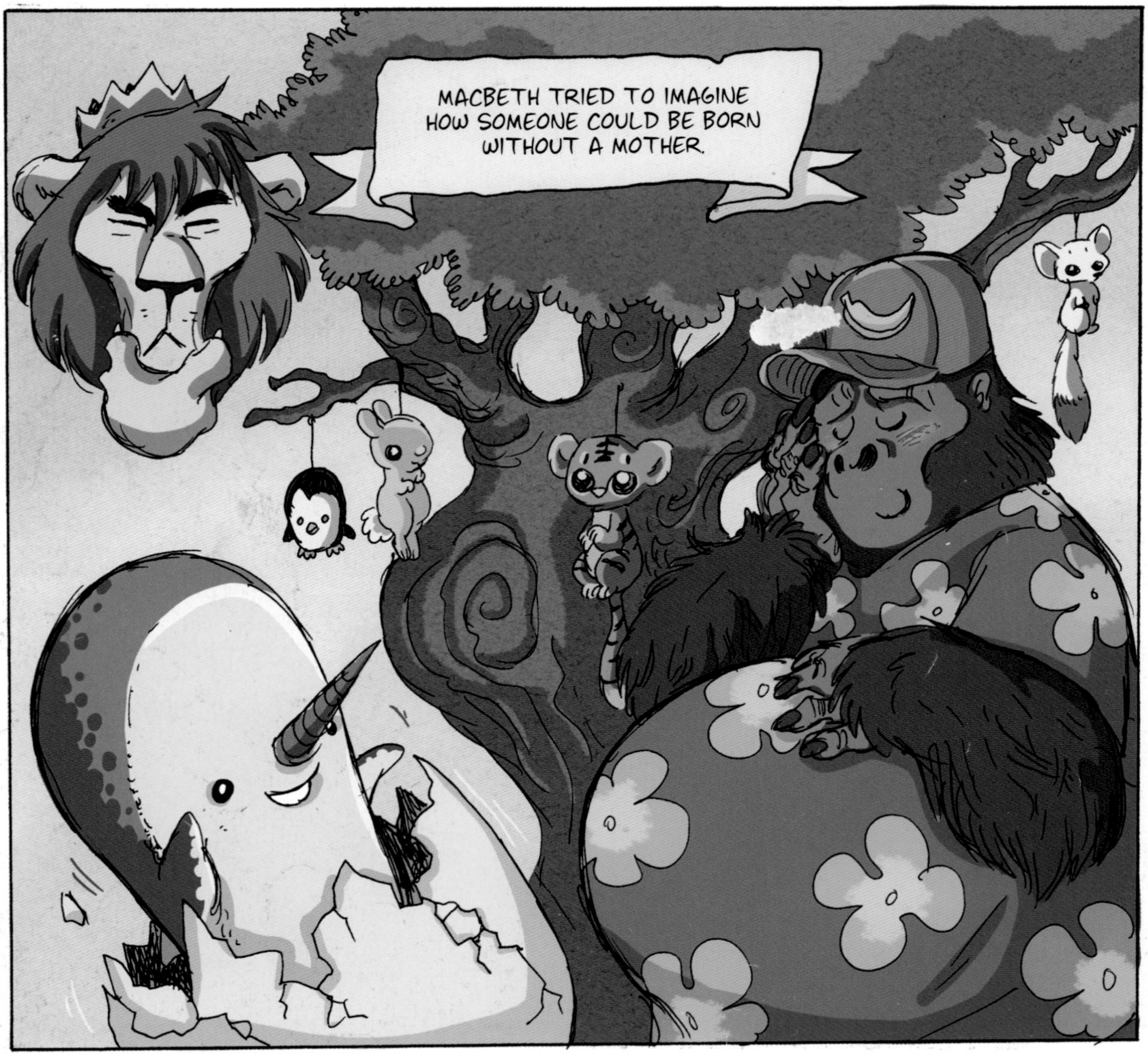
MACBETH TRIED TO IMAGINE HOW SOMEONE COULD BE BORN WITHOUT A MOTHER.

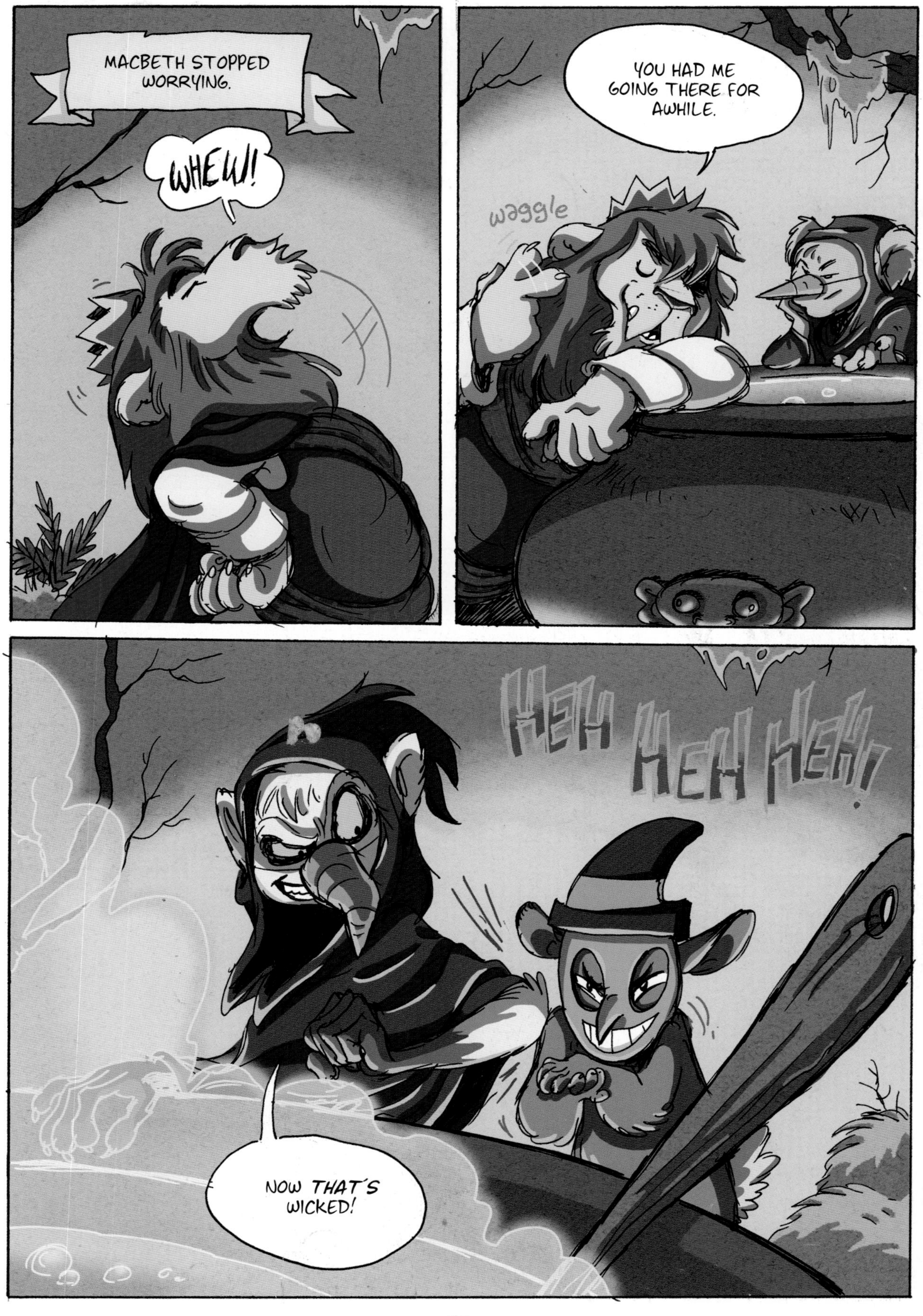
MACBETH STOPPED WORRYING.
WHEW!
YOU HAD ME GOING THERE FOR AWHILE.
waggle
HEH HEH HEH!
NOW THAT'S WICKED!

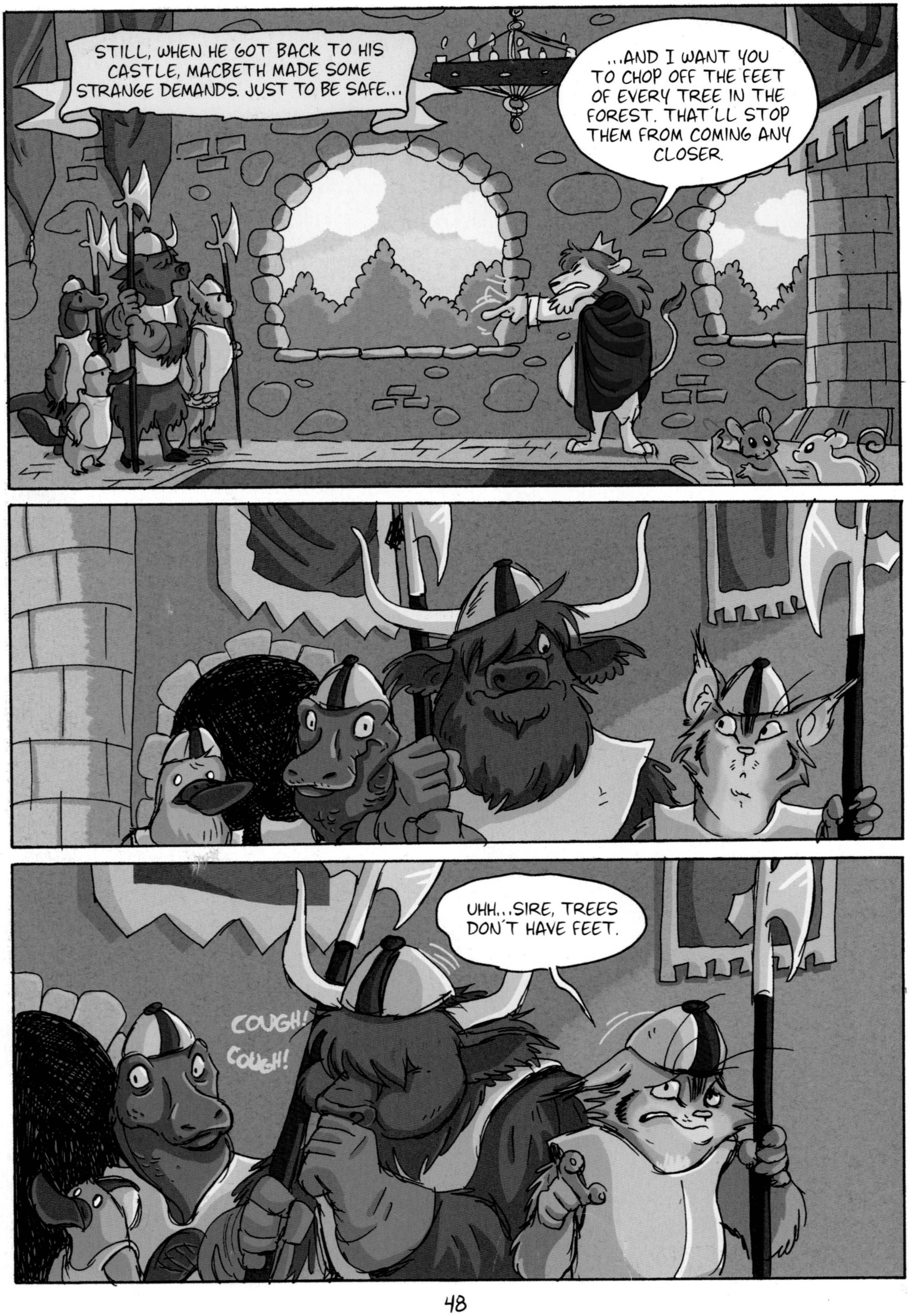
STILL, WHEN HE GOT BACK TO HIS CASTLE, MACBETH MADE SOME STRANGE DEMANDS. JUST TO BE SAFE...
...AND I WANT YOU TO CHOP OFF THE FEET OF EVERY TREE IN THE FOREST. THAT'LL STOP THEM FROM COMING ANY CLOSER.
UHH...SIRE, TREES DON'T HAVE FEET.
COUGH!
COUGH!

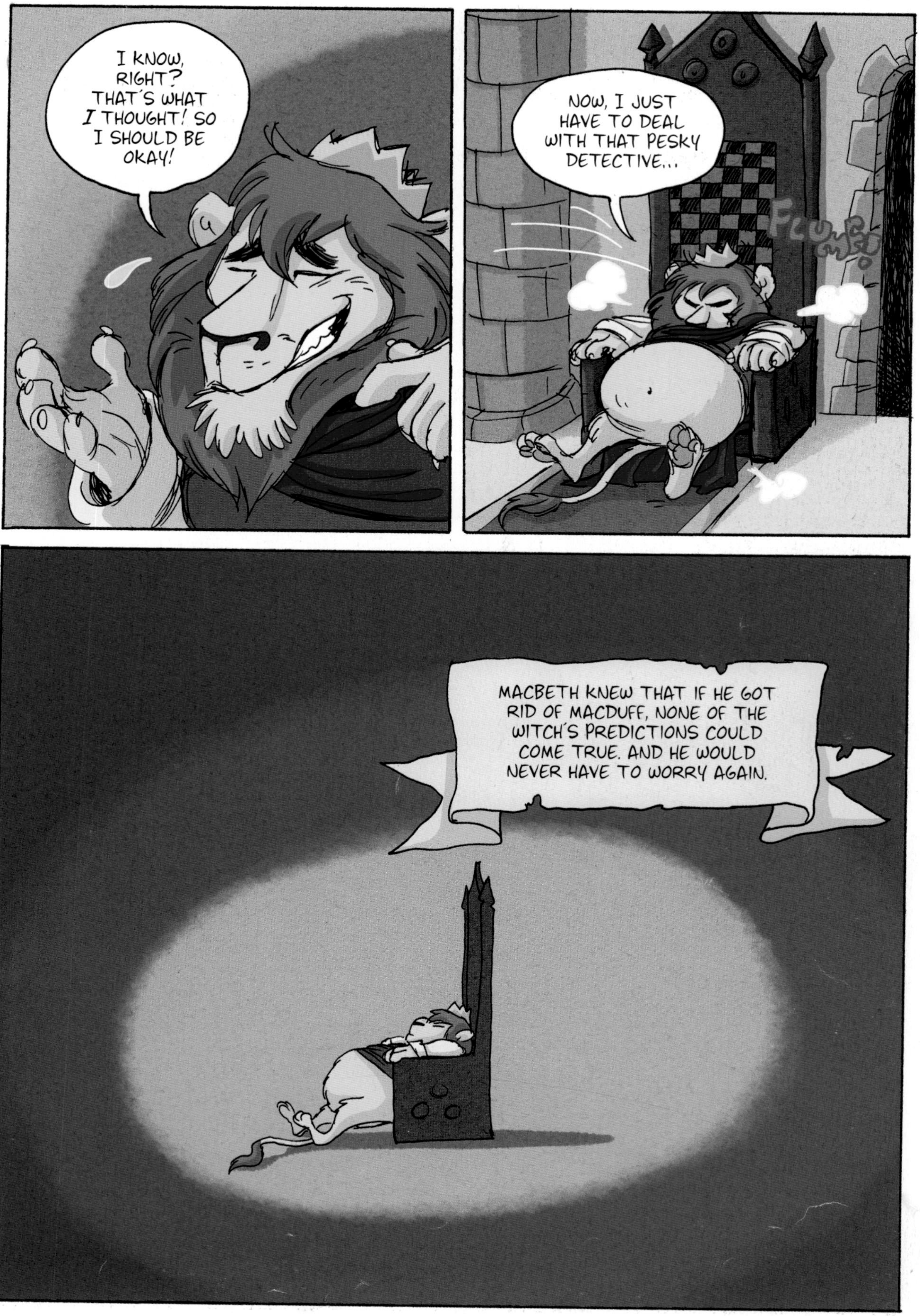
I KNOW, RIGHT? THAT'S WHAT *I* THOUGHT! SO I SHOULD BE OKAY!
NOW, I JUST HAVE TO DEAL WITH THAT PESKY DETECTIVE...
MACBETH KNEW THAT IF HE GOT RID OF MACDUFF, NONE OF THE WITCH'S PREDICTIONS COULD COME TRUE. AND HE WOULD NEVER HAVE TO WORRY AGAIN.

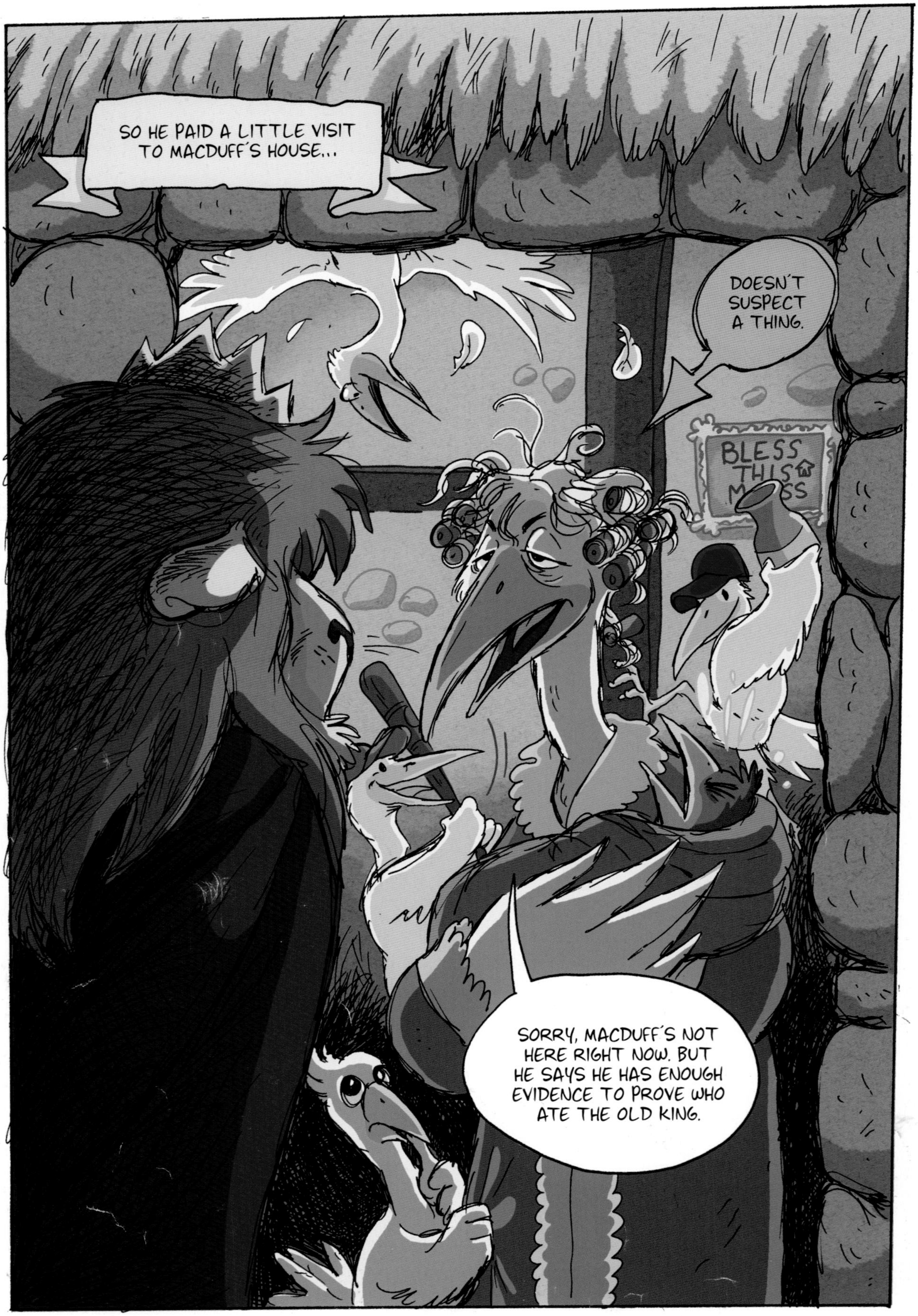
SO HE PAID A LITTLE VISIT TO MACDUFF'S HOUSE...
DOESN'T SUSPECT A THING.
BLESS THIS M ESS
SORRY, MACDUFF'S NOT HERE RIGHT NOW. BUT HE SAYS HE HAS ENOUGH EVIDENCE TO PROVE WHO ATE THE OLD KING.

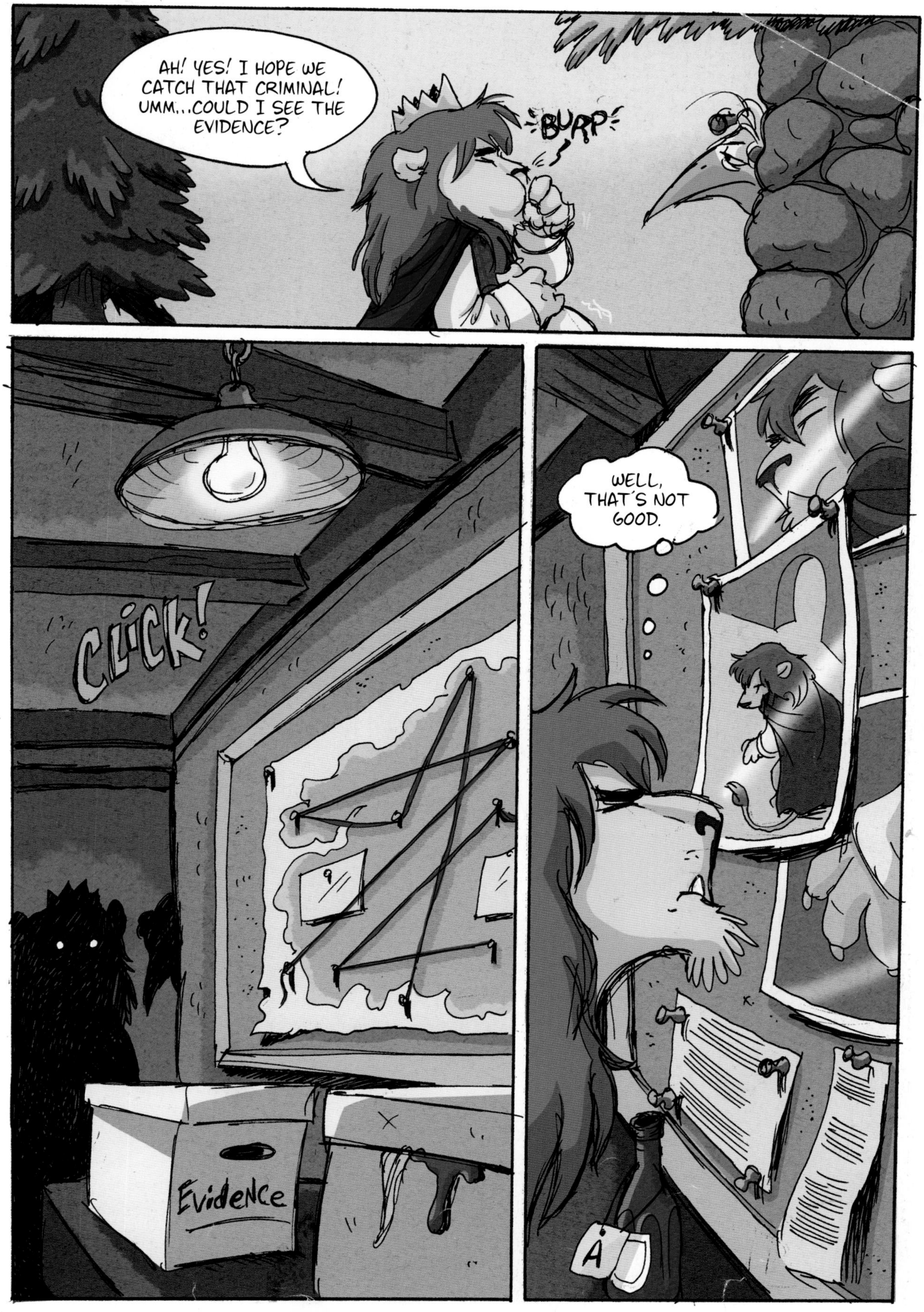
AH! YES! I HOPE WE CATCH THAT CRIMINAL! UMM...COULD I SEE THE EVIDENCE?
BURP
CLICK!
Evidence
WELL, THAT'S NOT GOOD.
A

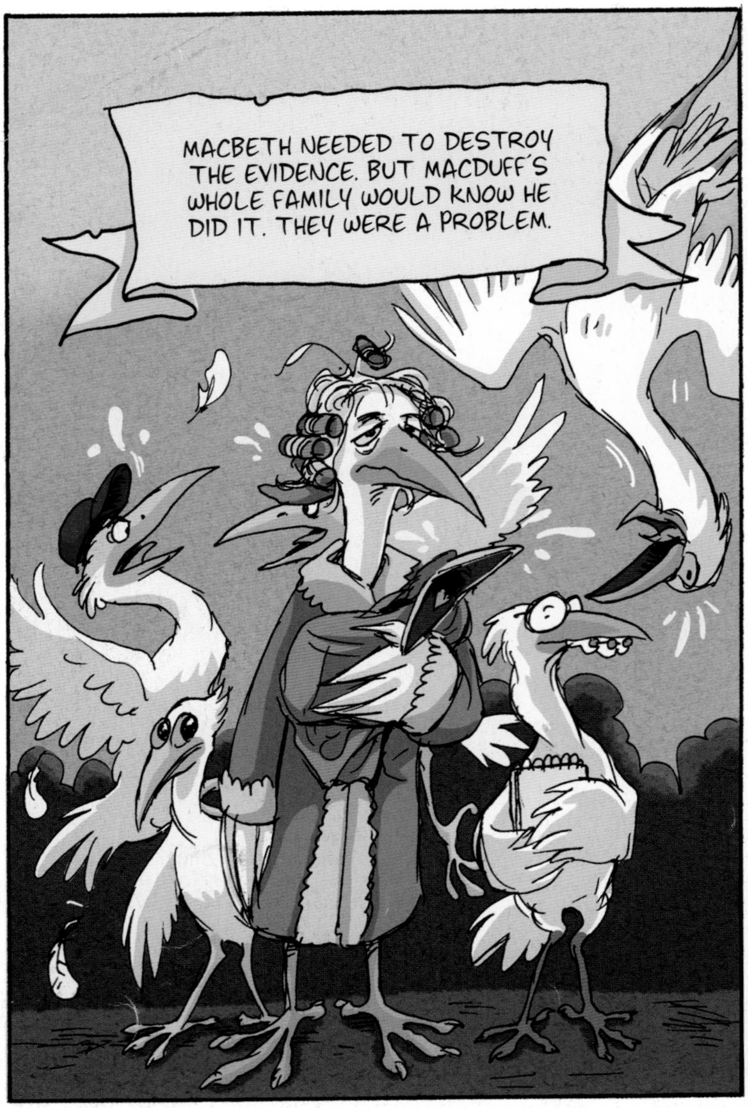
MACBETH NEEDED TO DESTROY THE EVIDENCE. BUT MACDUFF'S WHOLE FAMILY WOULD KNOW HE DID IT. THEY WERE A PROBLEM.

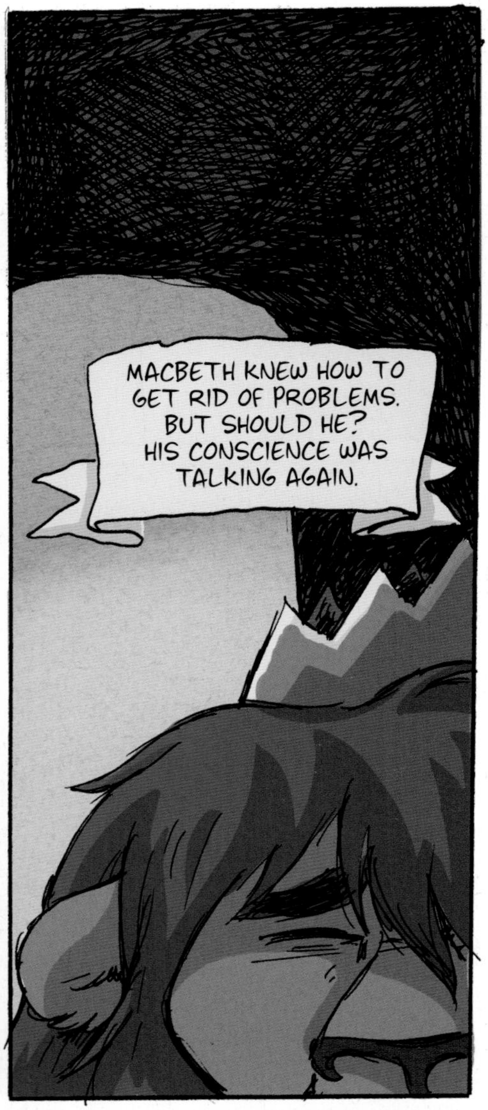
MACBETH KNEW HOW TO GET RID OF PROBLEMS. BUT SHOULD HE? HIS CONSCIENCE WAS TALKING AGAIN.

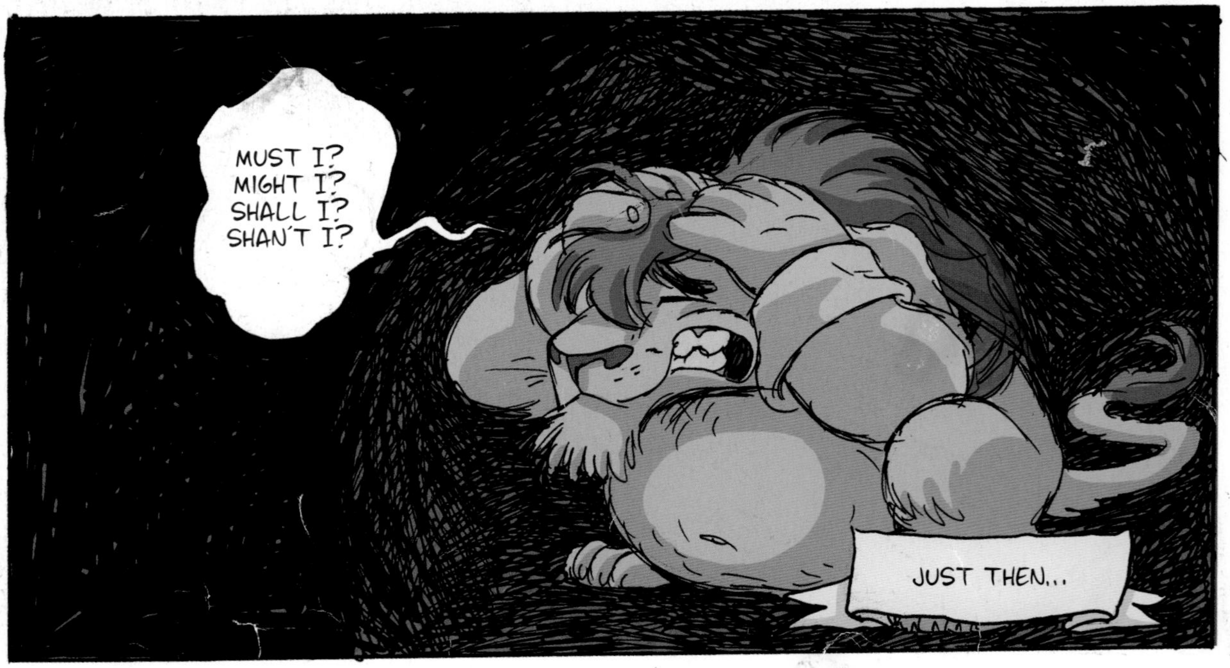
MUST I? MIGHT I? SHALL I? SHAN'T I?
JUST THEN...

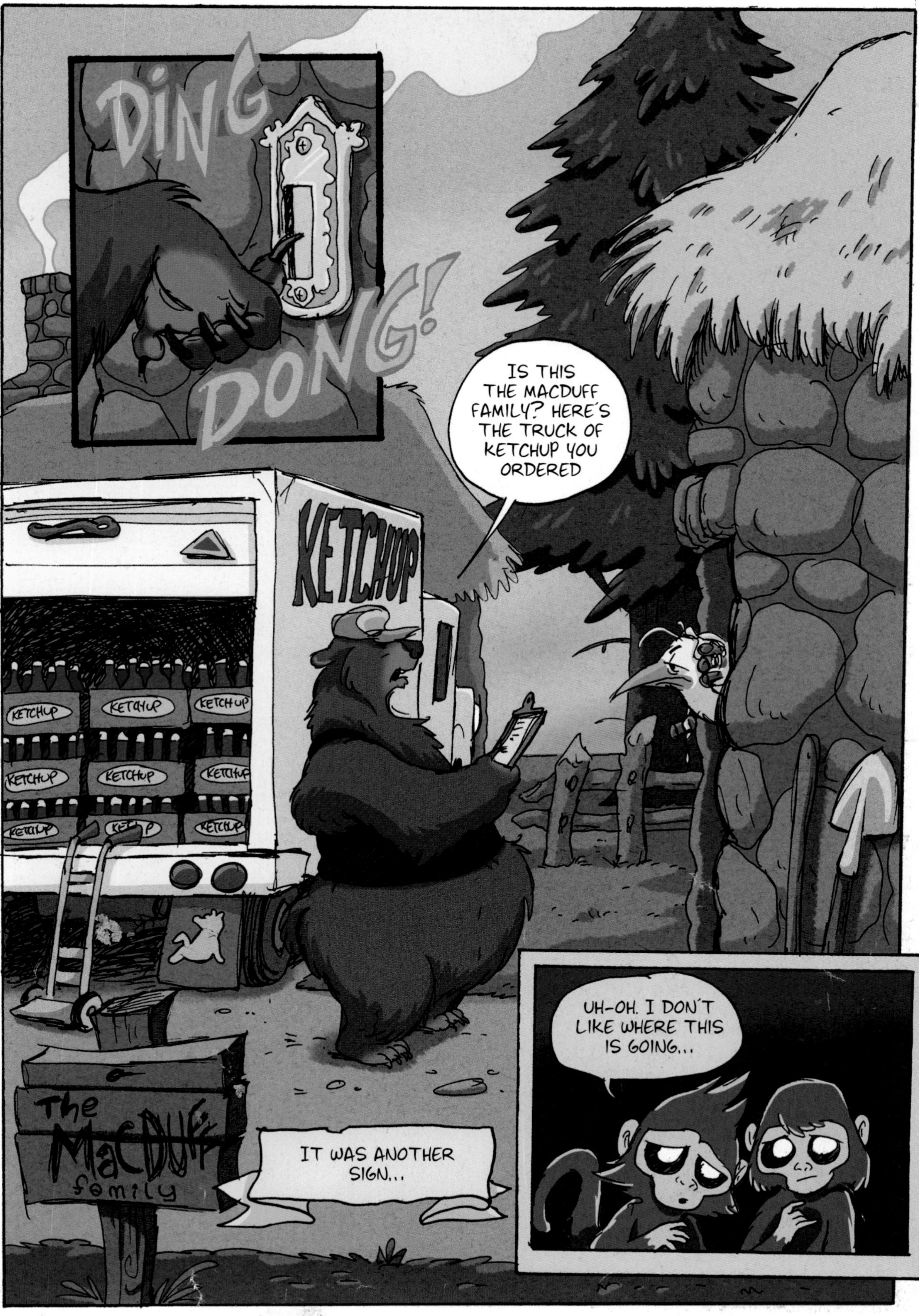
DING
DONG!
KETCHUP
IS THIS THE MACDUFF FAMILY? HERE'S THE TRUCK OF KETCHUP YOU ORDERED
The MacDuff family
IT WAS ANOTHER SIGN...
UH-OH. I DON'T LIKE WHERE THIS IS GOING...

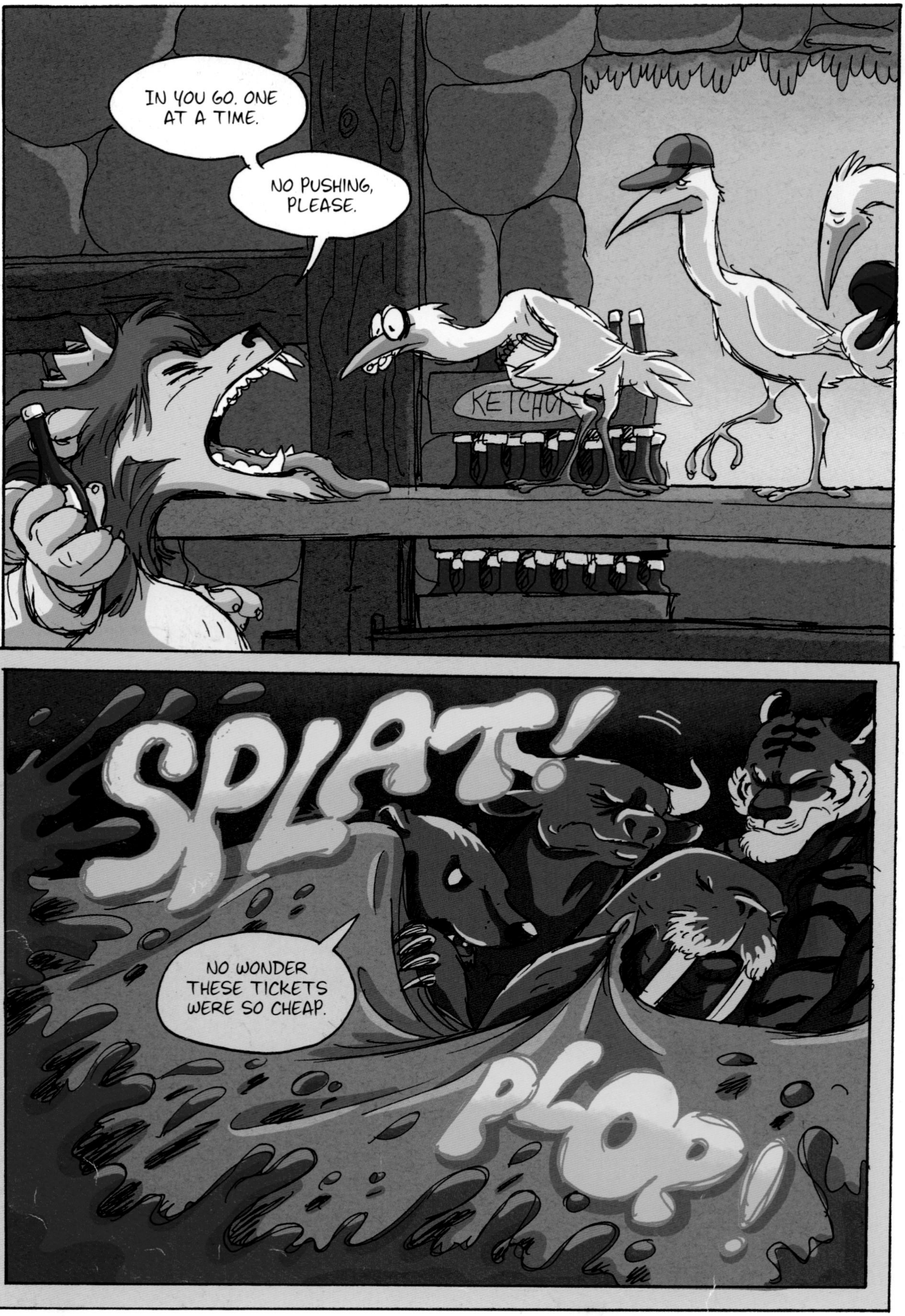
IN YOU GO. ONE AT A TIME.
NO PUSHING, PLEASE.
KETCHU
SPLAT!
NO WONDER THESE TICKETS WERE SO CHEAP.
PLOP!

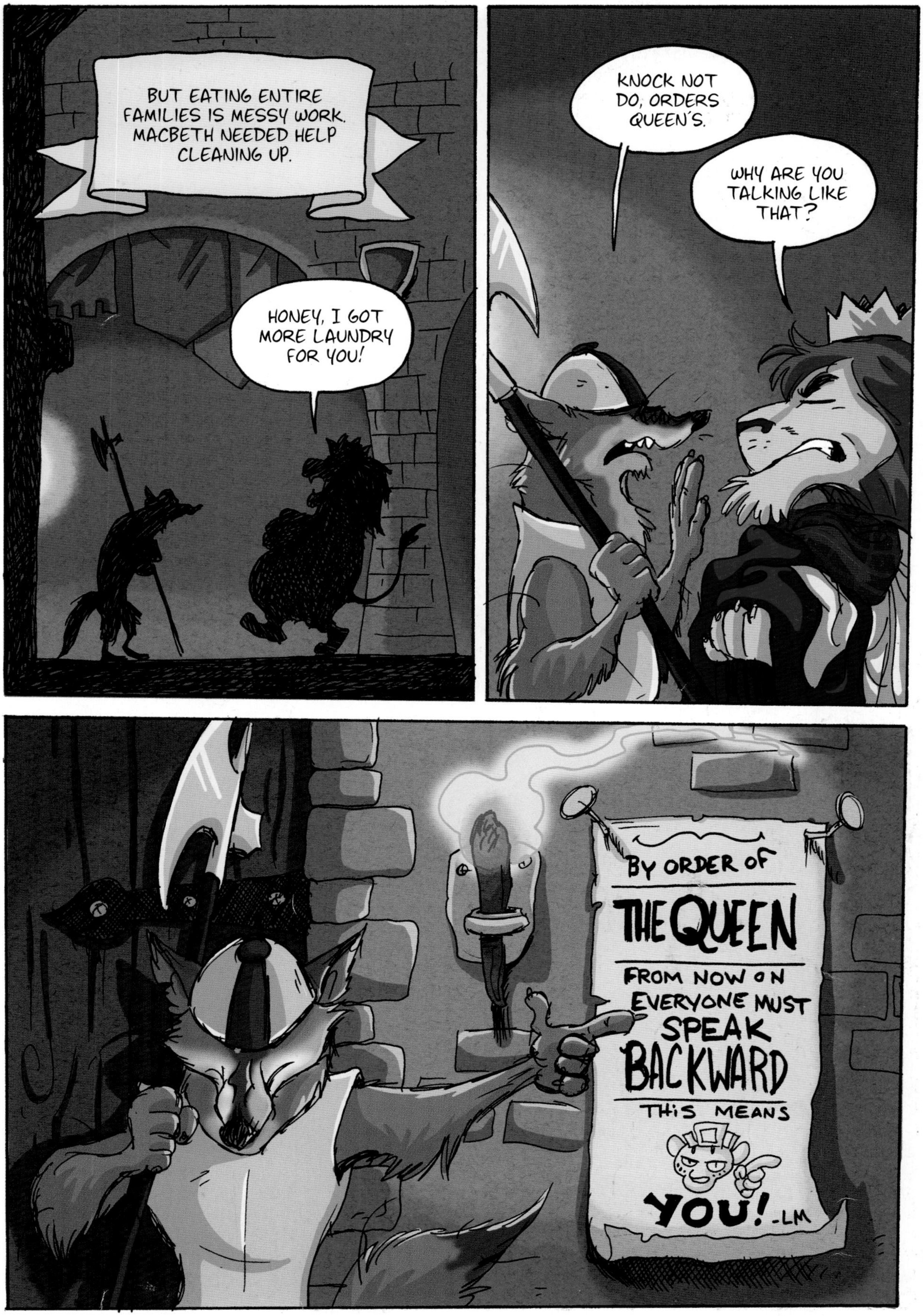
BUT EATING ENTIRE FAMILIES IS MESSY WORK. MACBETH NEEDED HELP CLEANING UP.
HONEY, I GOT MORE LAUNDRY FOR YOU!
KNOCK NOT DO, ORDERS QUEEN'S.
WHY ARE YOU TALKING LIKE THAT?
BY ORDER OF
THE QUEEN
FROM NOW ON EVERYONE MUST SPEAK BACKWARD
THIS MEANS
YOU! -LM

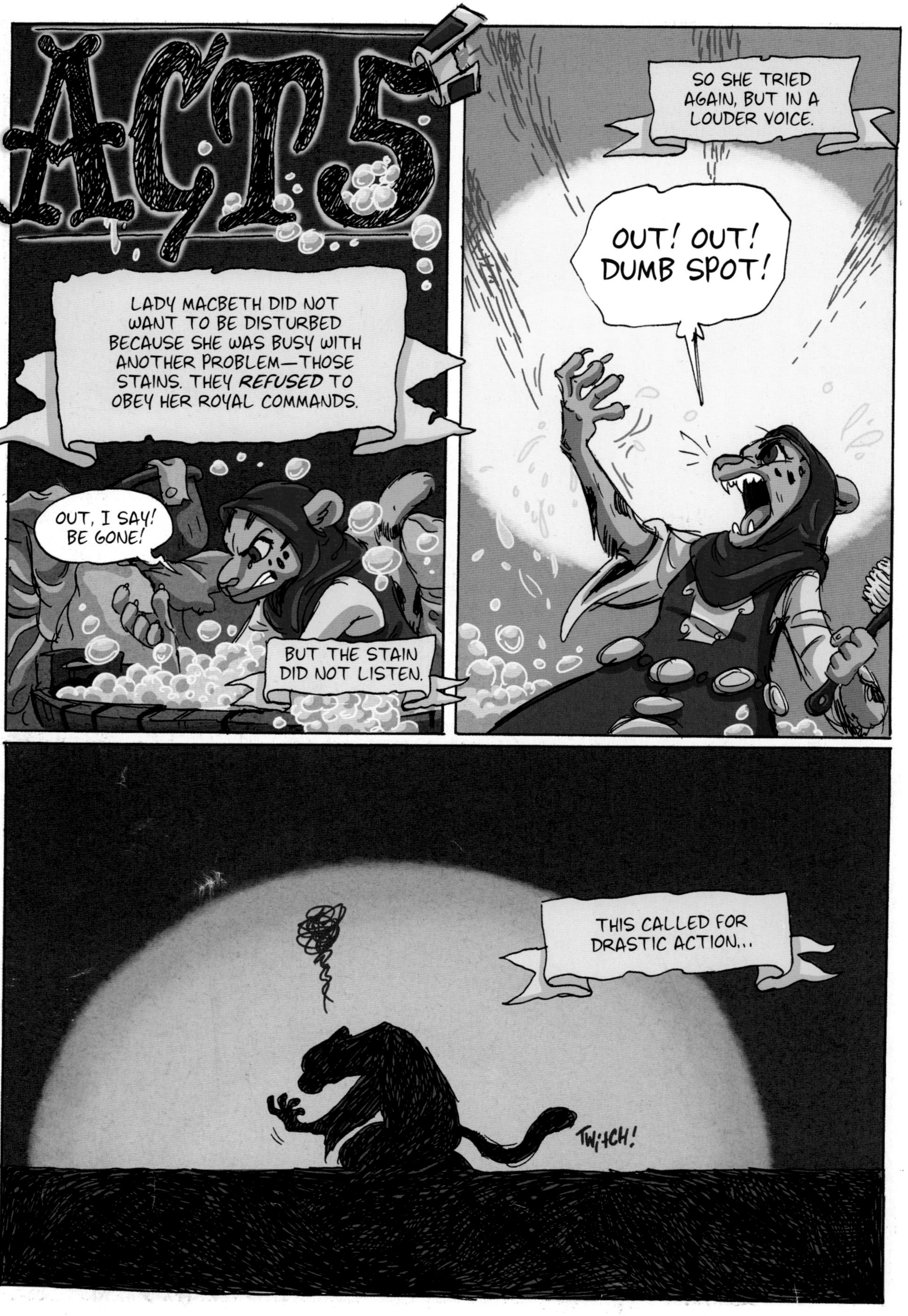
ACT 5
LADY MACBETH DID NOT WANT TO BE DISTURBED BECAUSE SHE WAS BUSY WITH ANOTHER PROBLEM—THOSE STAINS. THEY *REFUSED* TO OBEY HER ROYAL COMMANDS.
OUT, I SAY! BE GONE!
BUT THE STAIN DID NOT LISTEN.
SO SHE TRIED AGAIN, BUT IN A LOUDER VOICE.
OUT! OUT! DUMB SPOT!
THIS CALLED FOR DRASTIC ACTION...
TWITCH!

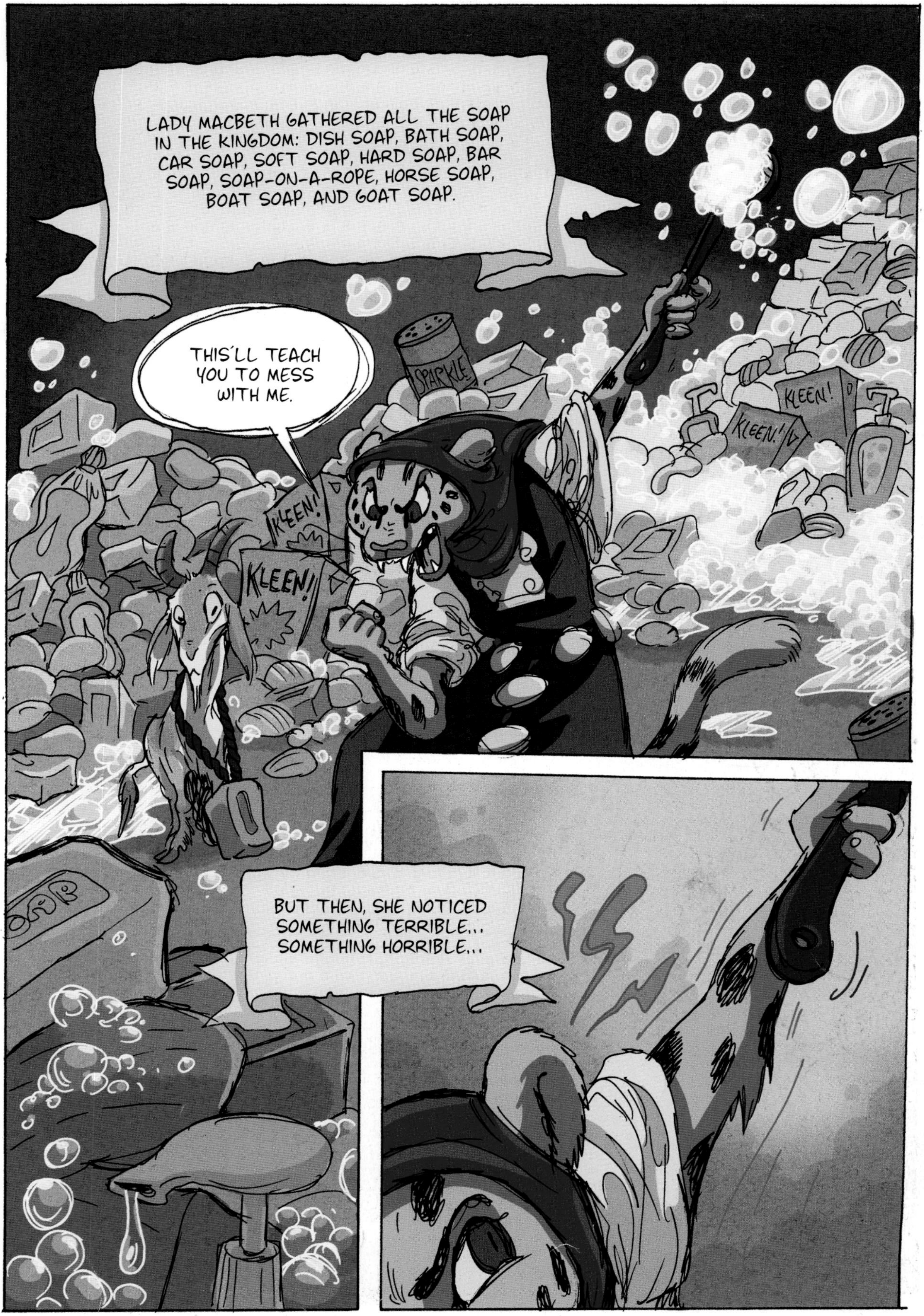
LADY MACBETH GATHERED ALL THE SOAP IN THE KINGDOM: DISH SOAP, BATH SOAP, CAR SOAP, SOFT SOAP, HARD SOAP, BAR SOAP, SOAP-ON-A-ROPE, HORSE SOAP, BOAT SOAP, AND GOAT SOAP.
THIS'LL TEACH YOU TO MESS WITH ME.
SPARKLE
KLEEN!
KLEEN!
KLEEN!
KLEEN!
BUT THEN, SHE NOTICED SOMETHING TERRIBLE... SOMETHING HORRIBLE...

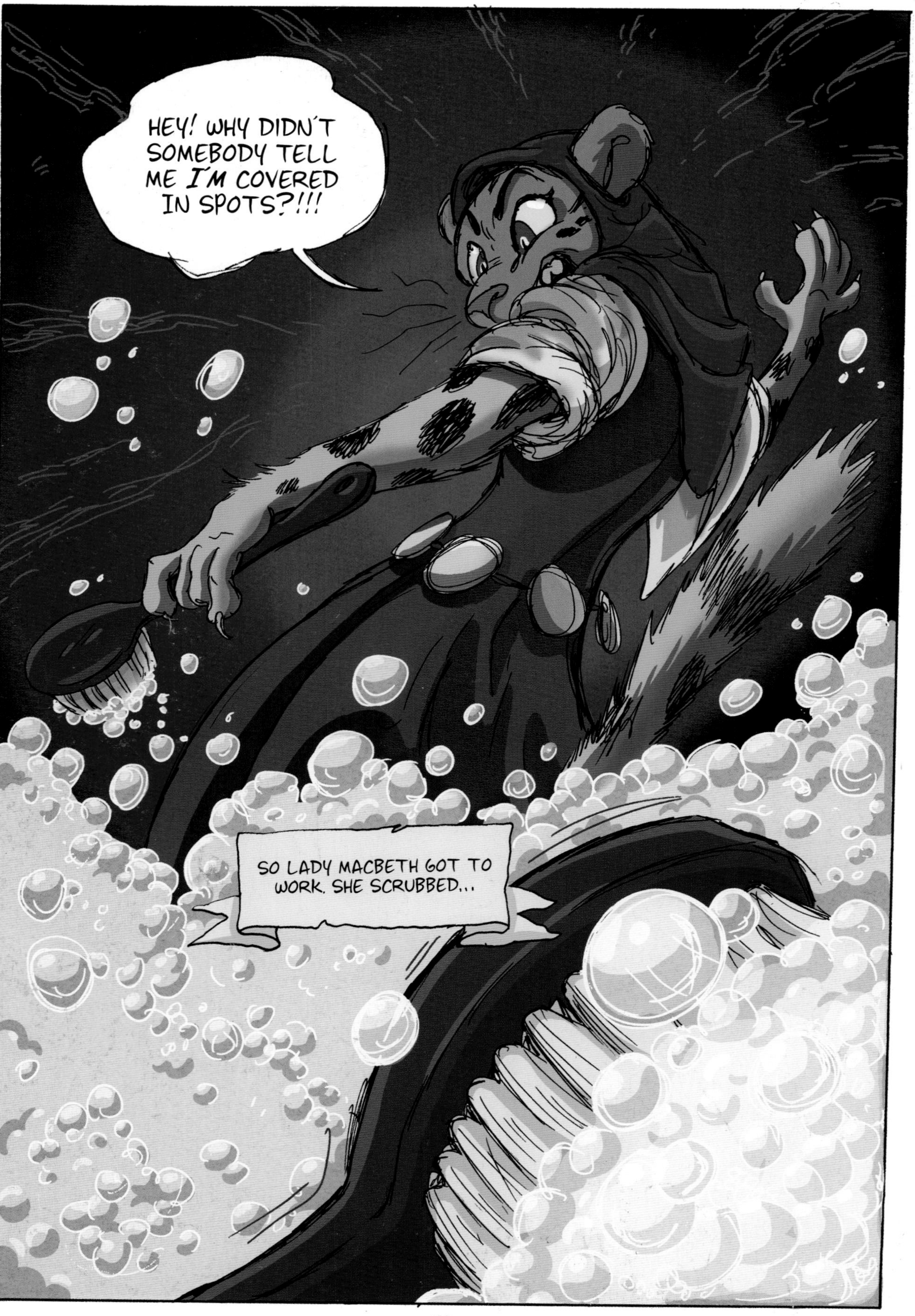
HEY! WHY DIDN'T SOMEBODY TELL ME *I'M* COVERED IN SPOTS?!!!
SO LADY MACBETH GOT TO WORK. SHE SCRUBBED...

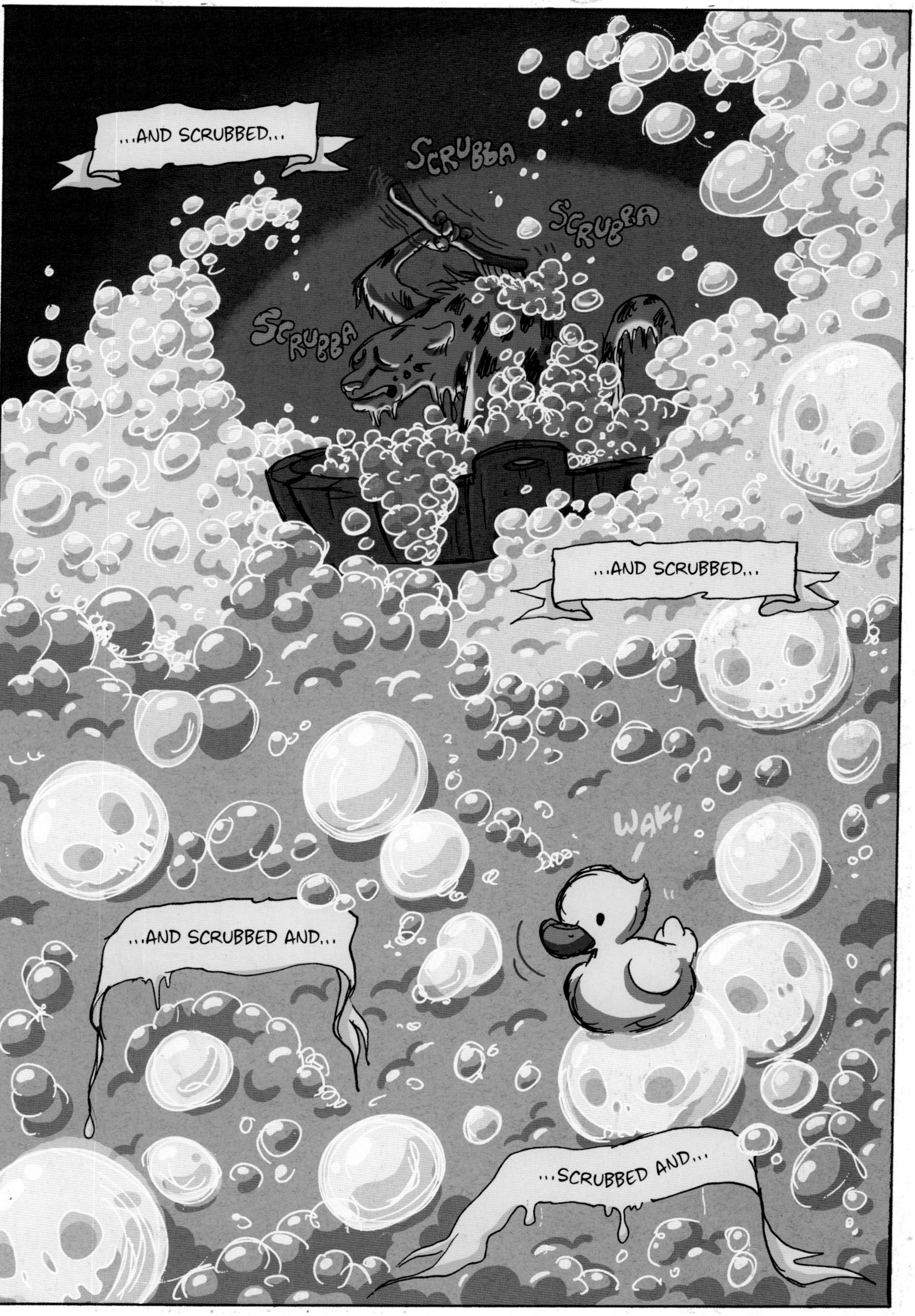
...AND SCRUBBED...
SCRUBBA
SCRUBBA
SCRUBBA
...AND SCRUBBED...
WAK!
...AND SCRUBBED AND...
...SCRUBBED AND...

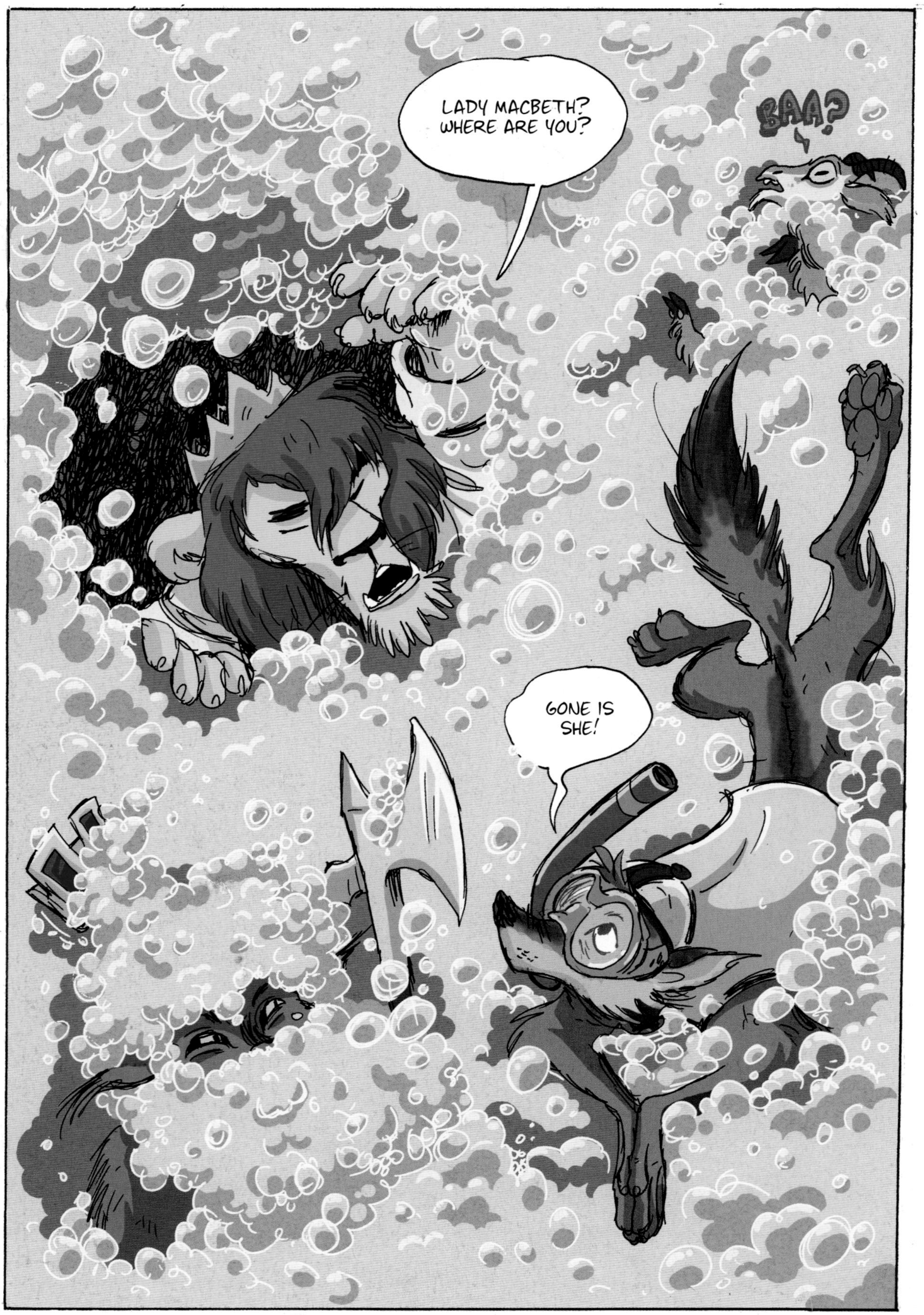
LADY MACBETH?
WHERE ARE YOU?
BAA?
GONE IS
SHE!

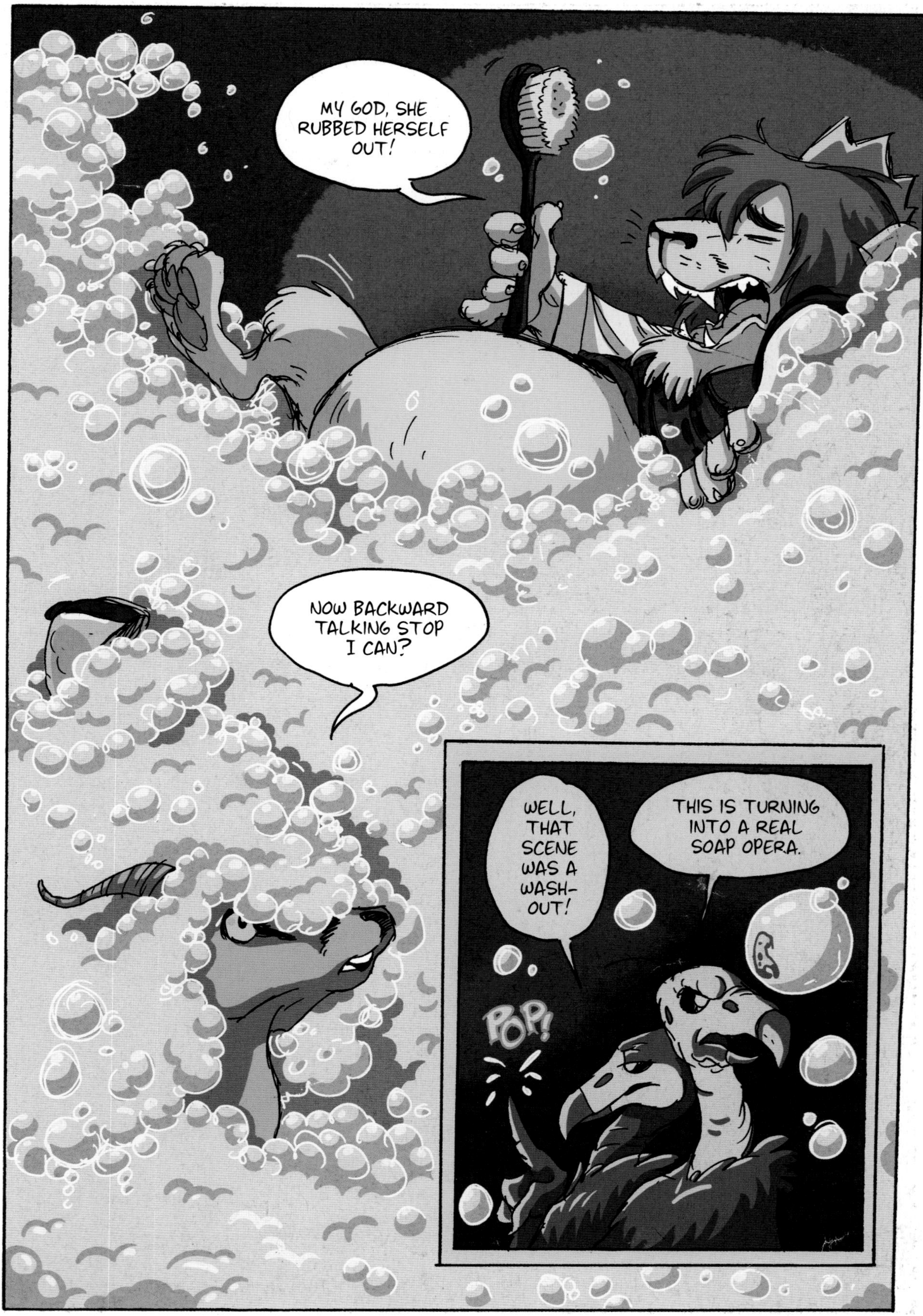
MY GOD, SHE RUBBED HERSELF OUT!
NOW BACKWARD TALKING STOP I CAN?
WELL, THAT SCENE WAS A WASH-OUT!
THIS IS TURNING INTO A REAL SOAP OPERA.
POP!

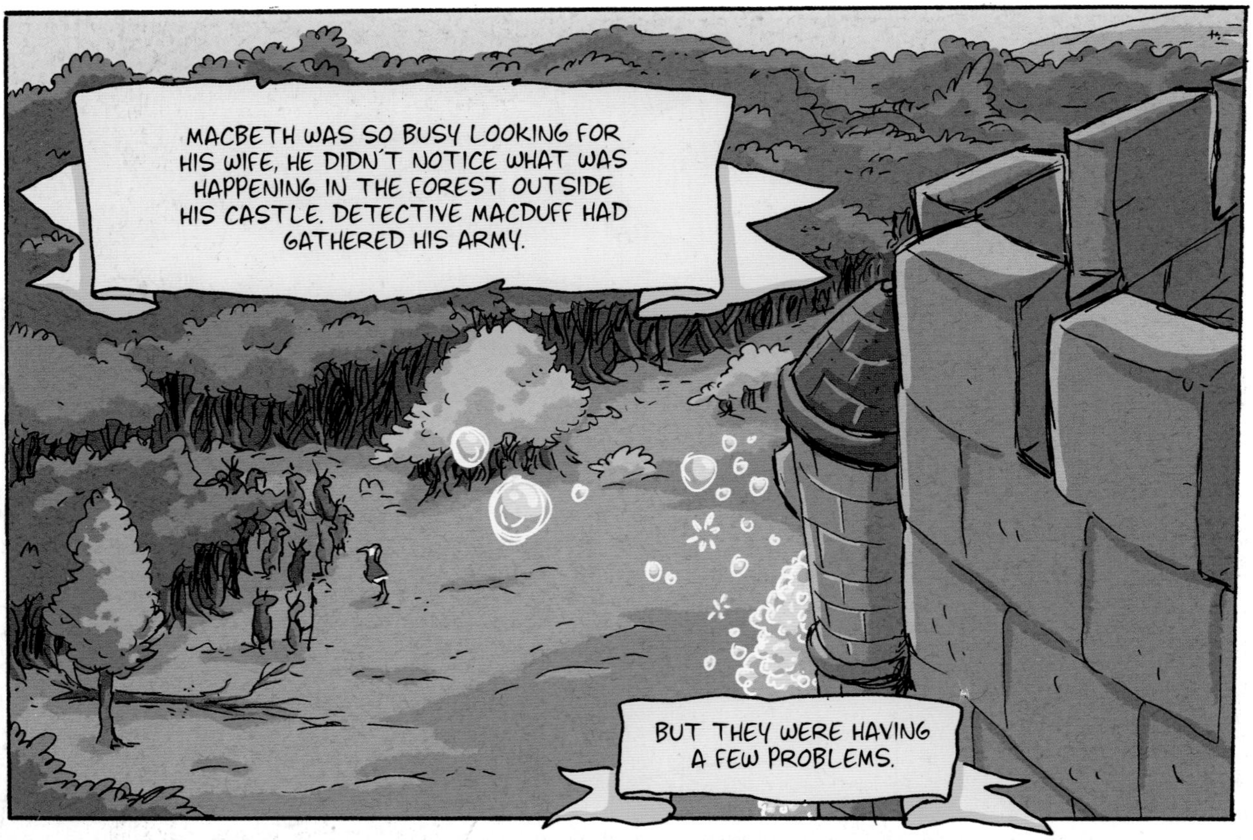
MACBETH WAS SO BUSY LOOKING FOR HIS WIFE, HE DIDN'T NOTICE WHAT WAS HAPPENING IN THE FOREST OUTSIDE HIS CASTLE. DETECTIVE MACDUFF HAD GATHERED HIS ARMY.
BUT THEY WERE HAVING A FEW PROBLEMS.

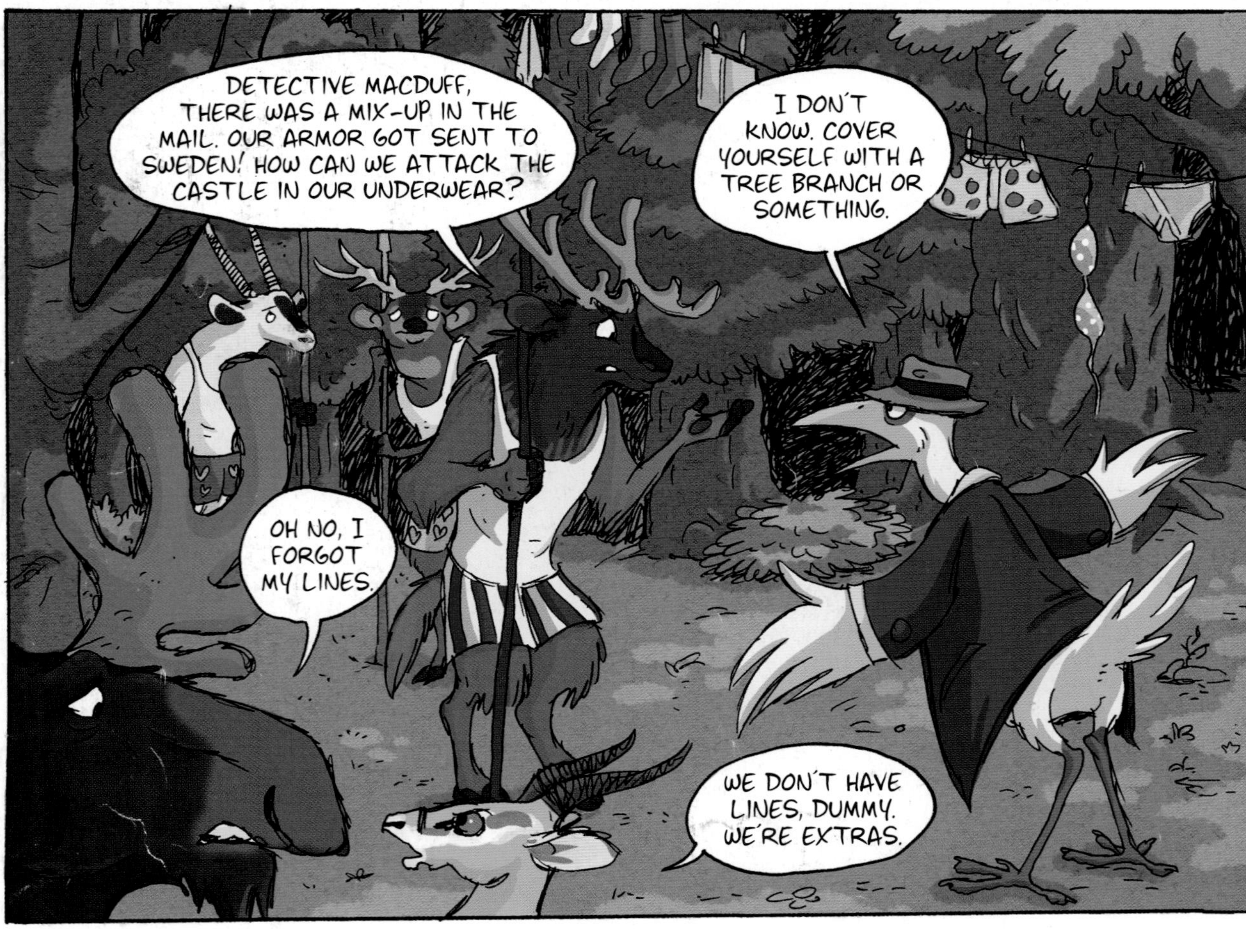
DETECTIVE MACDUFF, THERE WAS A MIX-UP IN THE MAIL. OUR ARMOR GOT SENT TO SWEDEN! HOW CAN WE ATTACK THE CASTLE IN OUR UNDERWEAR?
I DON'T KNOW. COVER YOURSELF WITH A TREE BRANCH OR SOMETHING.
OH NO, I FORGOT MY LINES.
WE DON'T HAVE LINES, DUMMY. WE'RE EXTRAS.

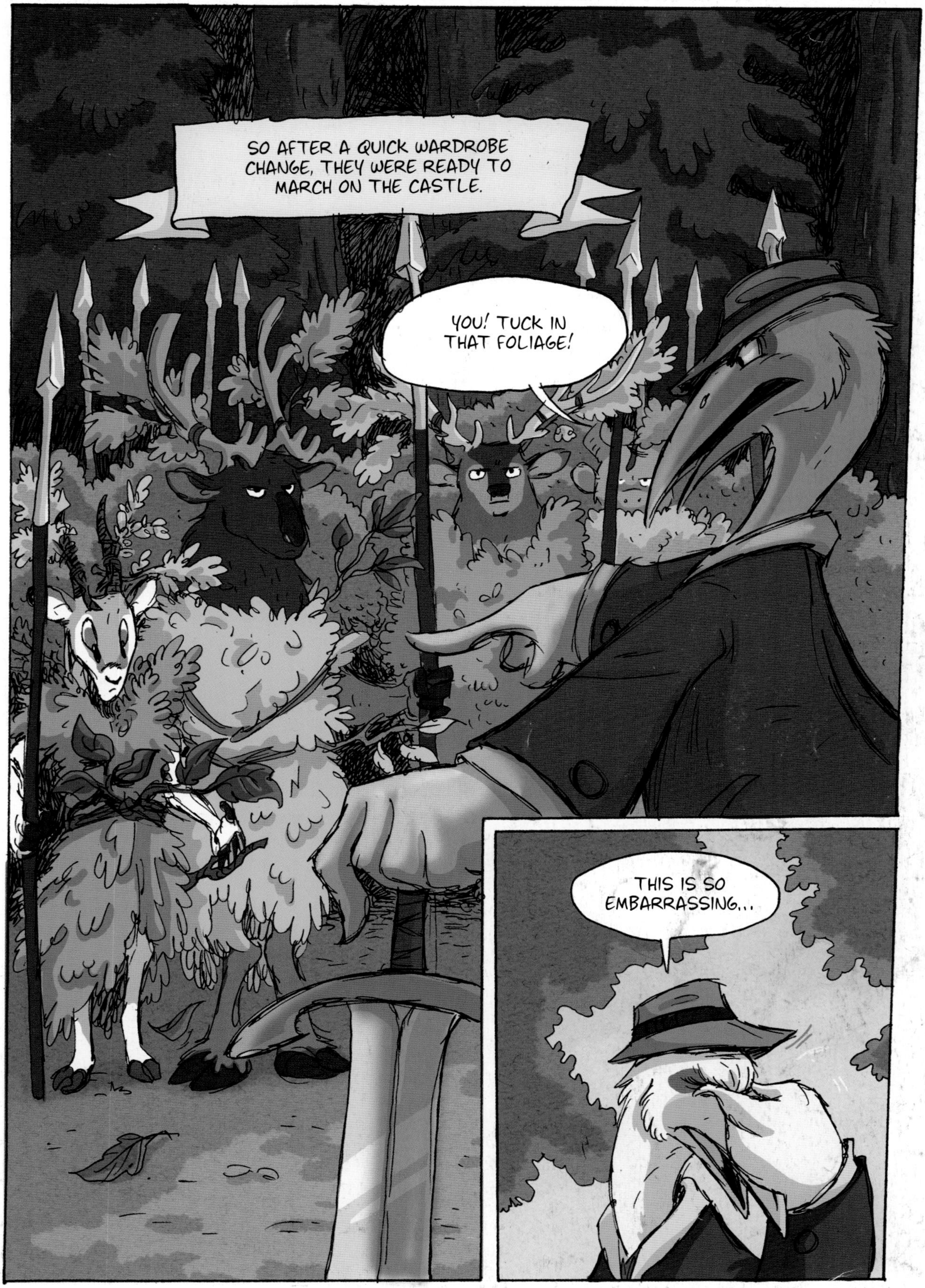
SO AFTER A QUICK WARDROBE CHANGE, THEY WERE READY TO MARCH ON THE CASTLE.
YOU! TUCK IN THAT FOLIAGE!
THIS IS SO EMBARRASSING...

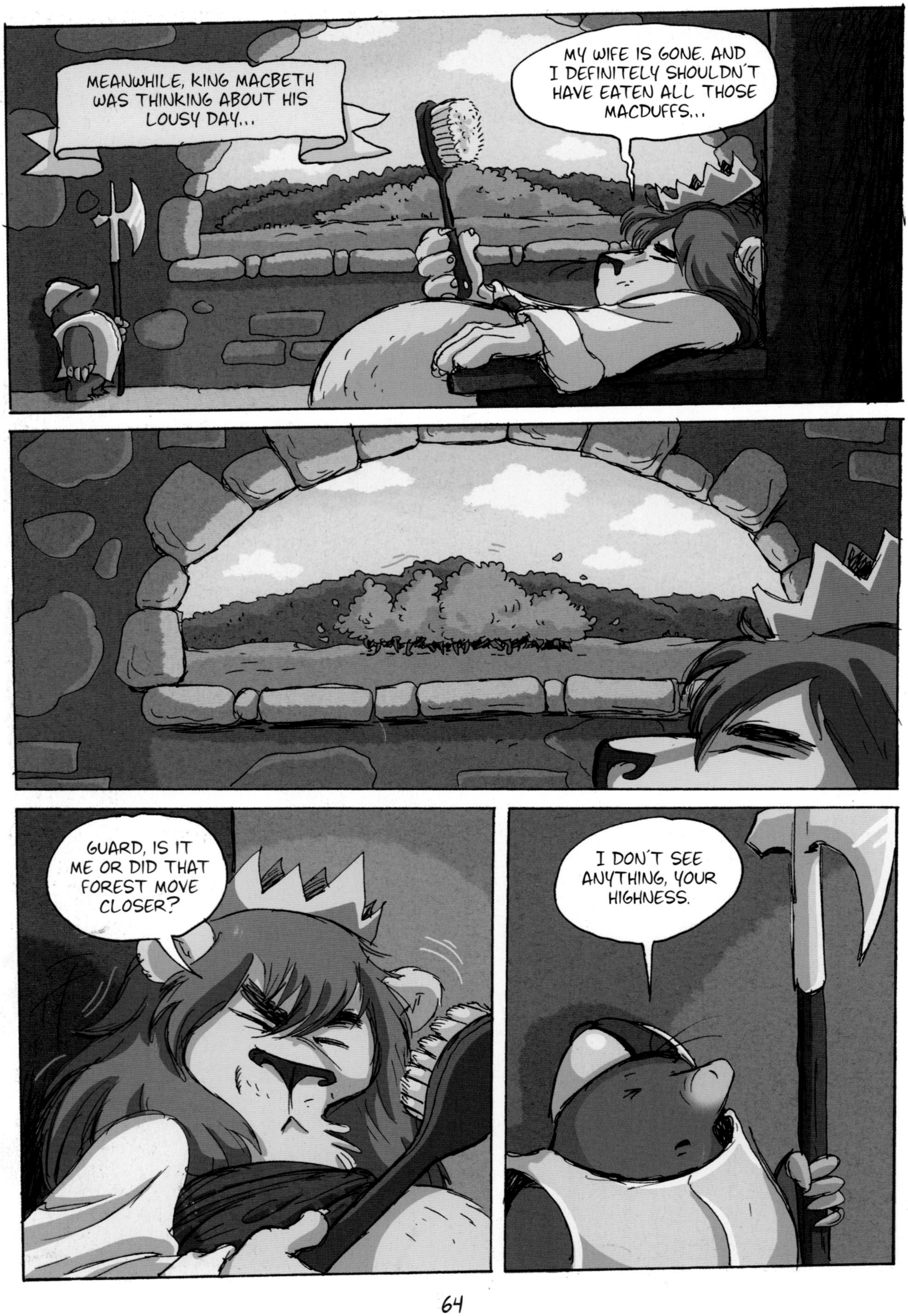
MEANWHILE, KING MACBETH WAS THINKING ABOUT HIS LOUSY DAY...
MY WIFE IS GONE. AND I DEFINITELY SHOULDN'T HAVE EATEN ALL THOSE MACDUFFS...
GUARD, IS IT ME OR DID THAT FOREST MOVE CLOSER?
I DON'T SEE ANYTHING, YOUR HIGHNESS.

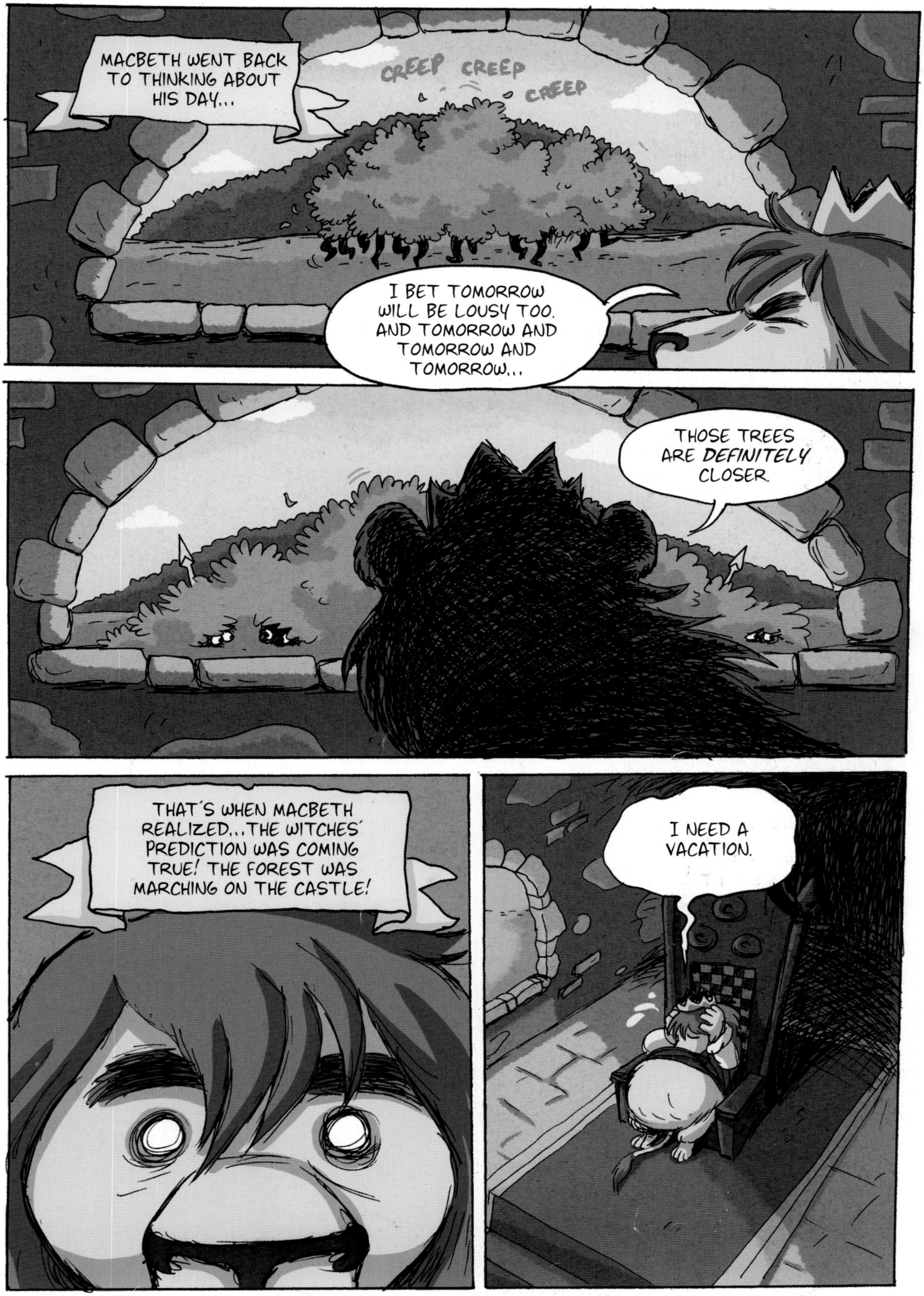
MACBETH WENT BACK TO THINKING ABOUT HIS DAY...
CREEP CREEP
CREEP
I BET TOMORROW WILL BE LOUSY TOO. AND TOMORROW AND TOMORROW AND TOMORROW...
THOSE TREES ARE *DEFINITELY* CLOSER.
THAT'S WHEN MACBETH REALIZED... THE WITCHES' PREDICTION WAS COMING TRUE! THE FOREST WAS MARCHING ON THE CASTLE!
I NEED A VACATION.

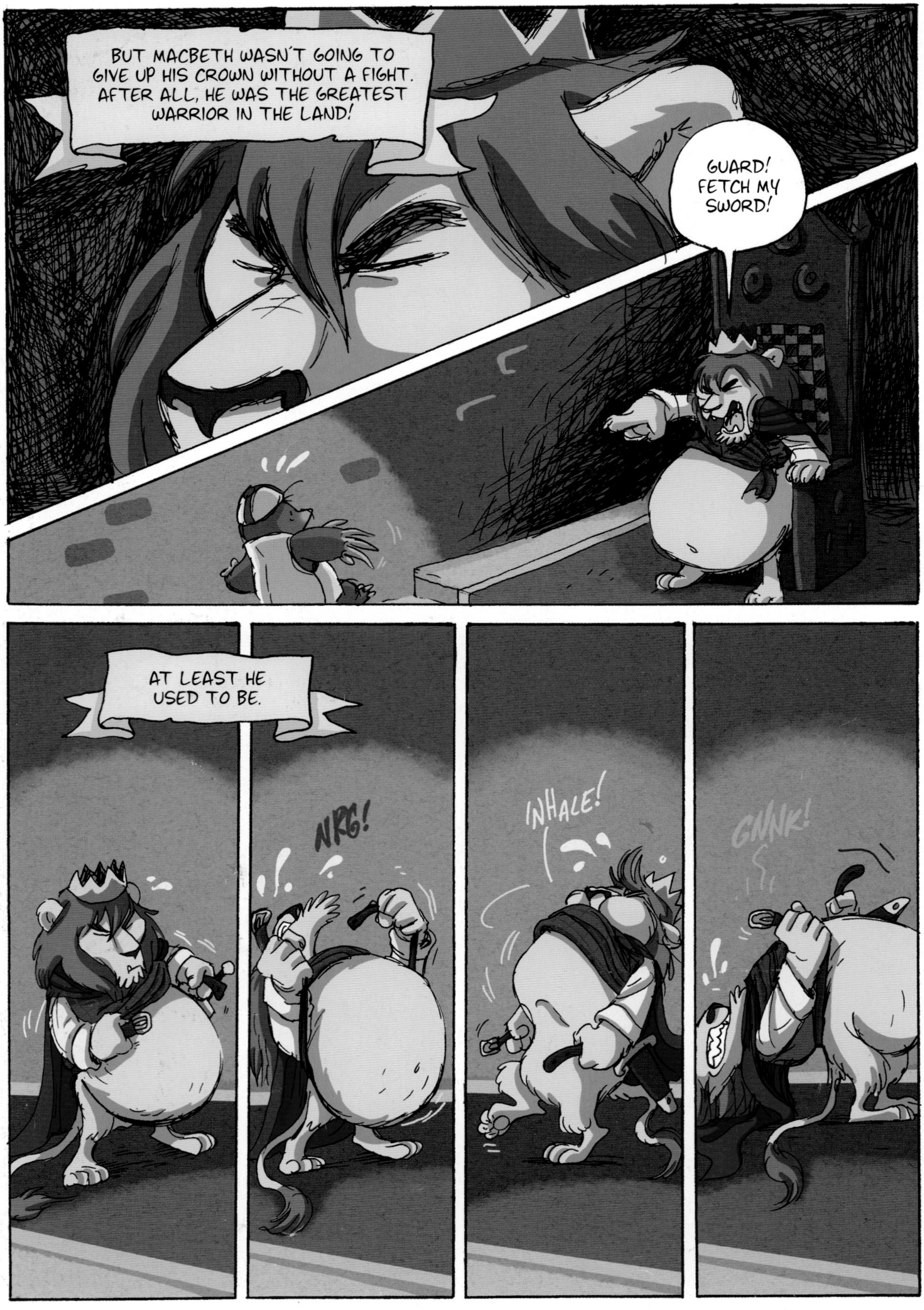

BUT MACBETH WASN'T GOING TO GIVE UP HIS CROWN WITHOUT A FIGHT. AFTER ALL, HE WAS THE GREATEST WARRIOR IN THE LAND!
GUARD! FETCH MY SWORD!
AT LEAST HE USED TO BE.
NRG!
INHALE!
GNNK!

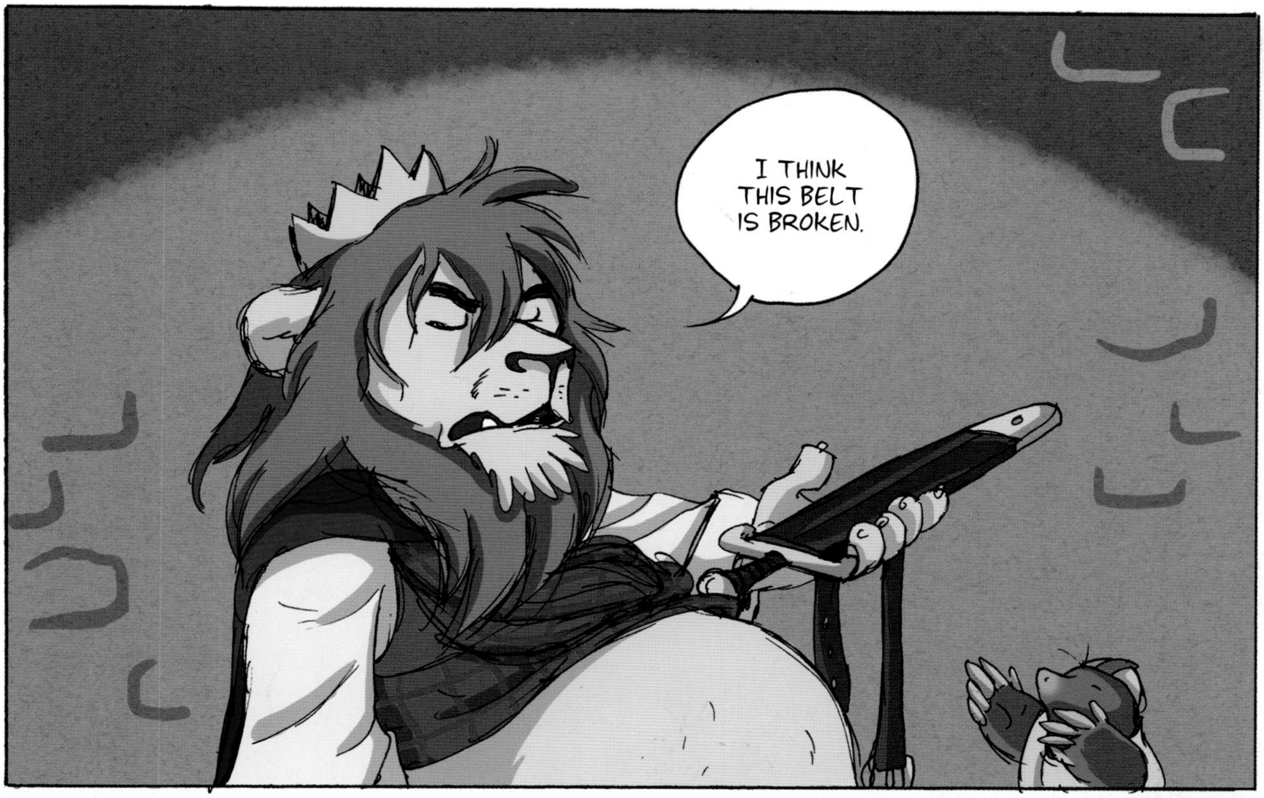
I THINK THIS BELT IS BROKEN.

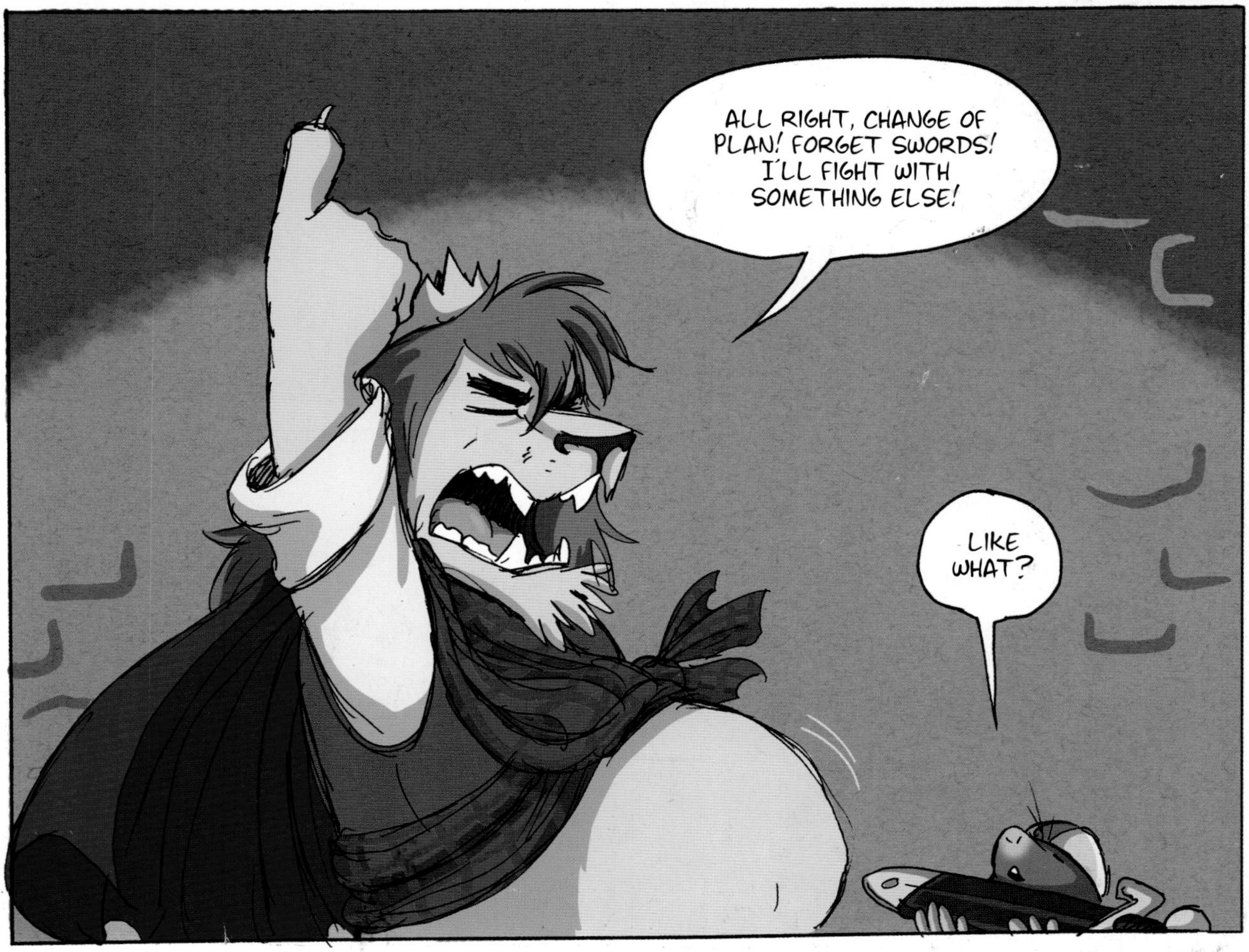
ALL RIGHT, CHANGE OF PLAN! FORGET SWORDS! I'LL FIGHT WITH SOMETHING ELSE!
LIKE WHAT?

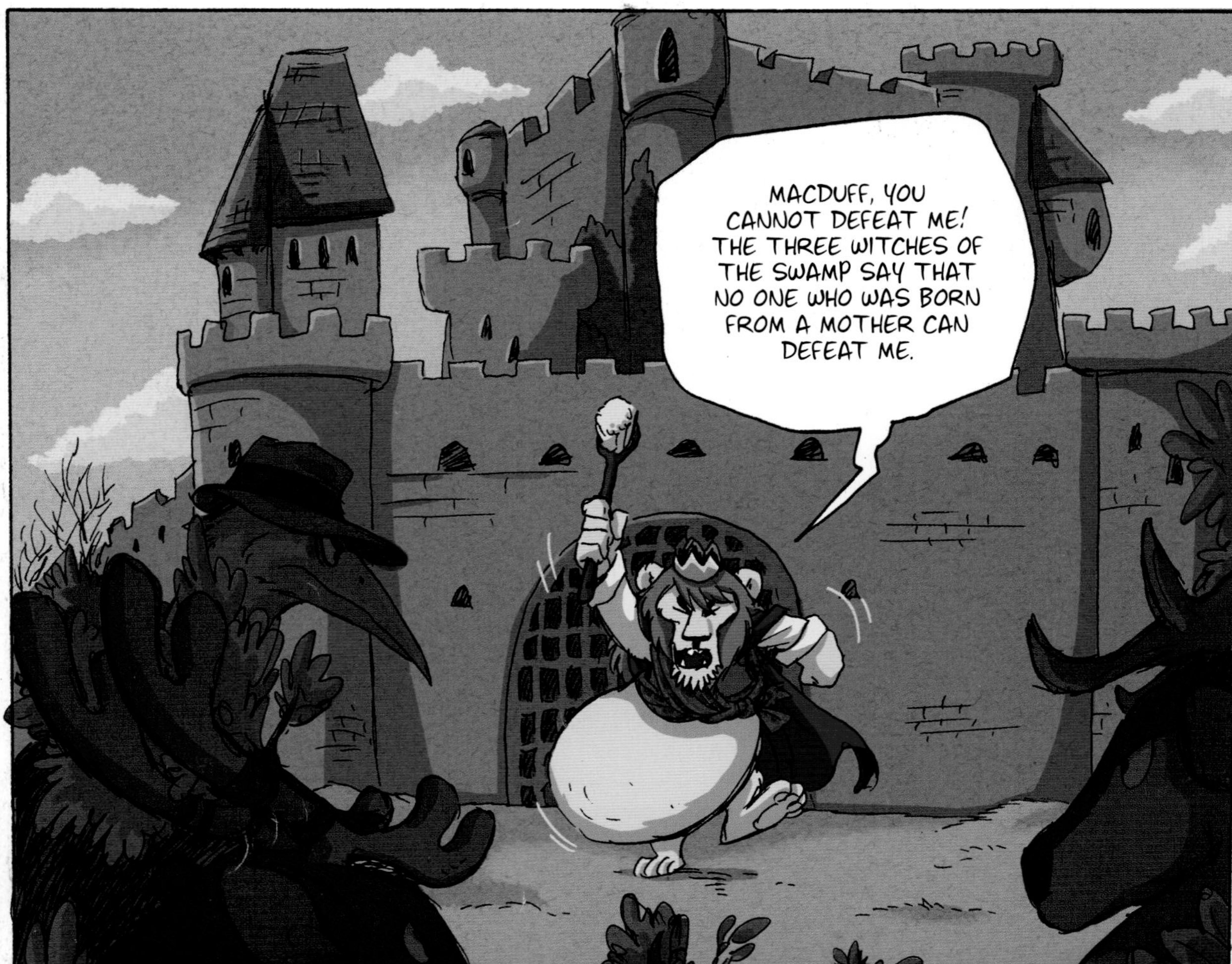
MACDUFF, YOU CANNOT DEFEAT ME! THE THREE WITCHES OF THE SWAMP SAY THAT NO ONE WHO WAS BORN FROM A MOTHER CAN DEFEAT ME.

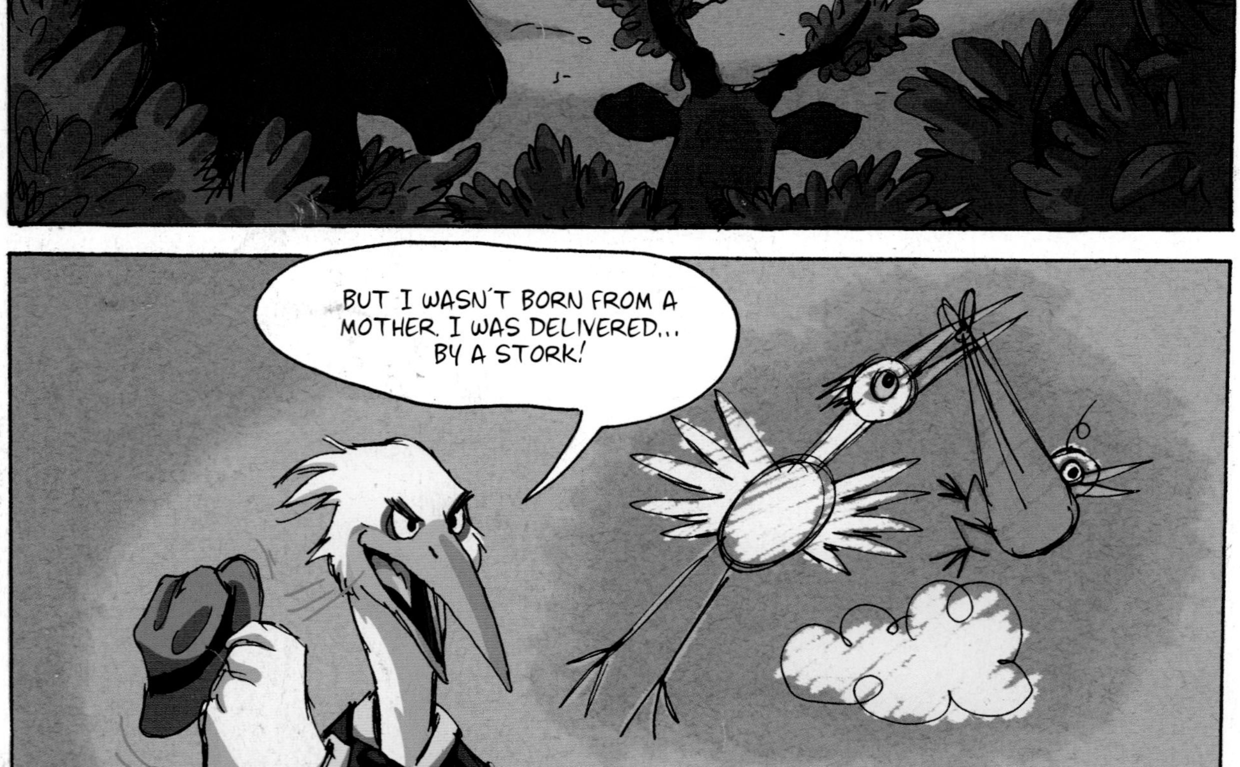
BUT I WASN´T BORN FROM A MOTHER. I WAS DELIVERED... BY A STORK!

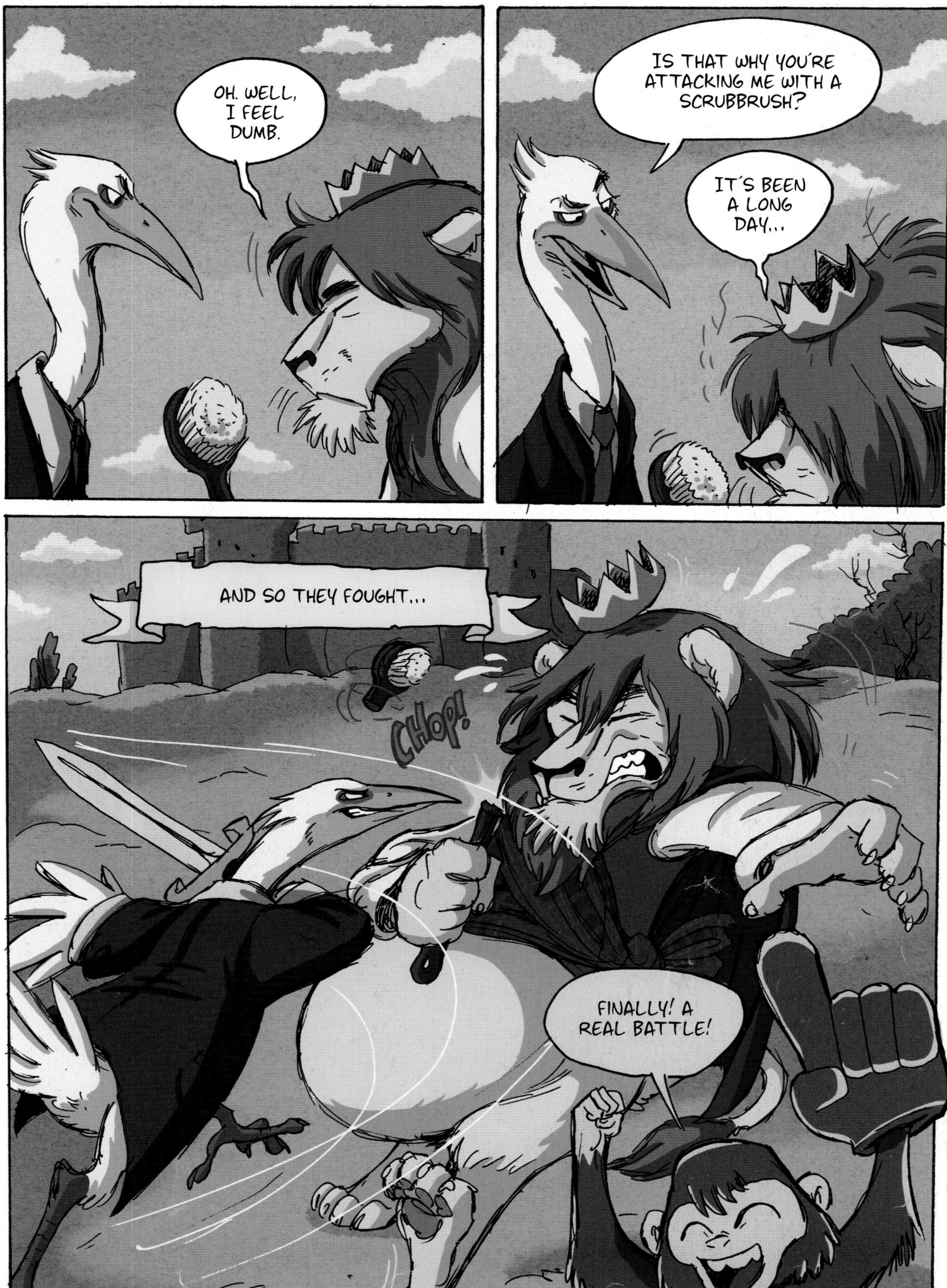
OH. WELL, I FEEL DUMB.
IS THAT WHY YOU'RE ATTACKING ME WITH A SCRUBBRUSH?
IT'S BEEN A LONG DAY...
AND SO THEY FOUGHT...
CHOP!
FINALLY! A REAL BATTLE!

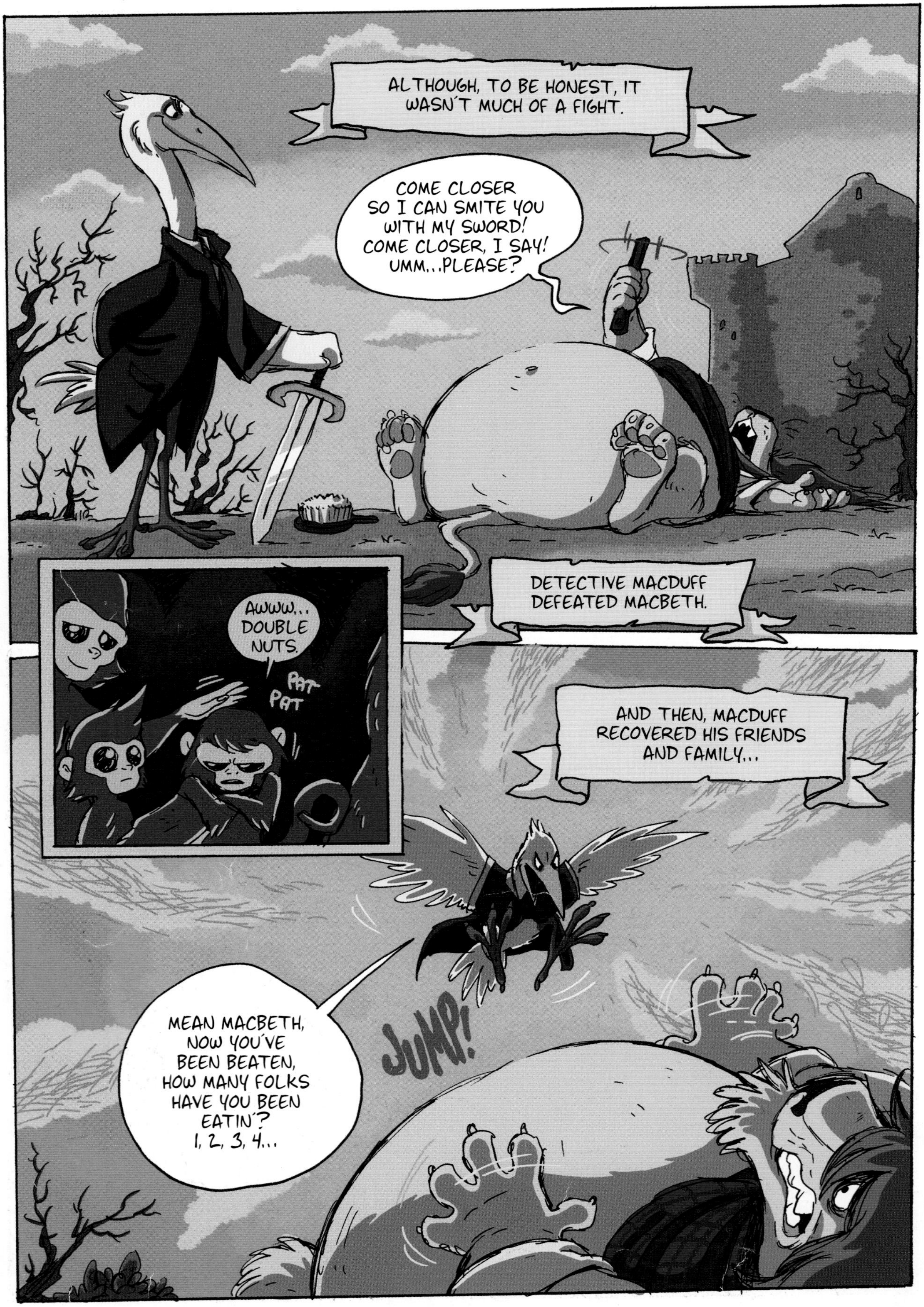
ALTHOUGH, TO BE HONEST, IT WASN'T MUCH OF A FIGHT.
COME CLOSER SO I CAN SMITE YOU WITH MY SWORD! COME CLOSER, I SAY! UMM...PLEASE?
DETECTIVE MACDUFF DEFEATED MACBETH.
AWWW... DOUBLE NUTS.
PAT PAT
AND THEN, MACDUFF RECOVERED HIS FRIENDS AND FAMILY...
MEAN MACBETH, NOW YOU'VE BEEN BEATEN, HOW MANY FOLKS HAVE YOU BEEN EATIN'? 1, 2, 3, 4...
JUMP!

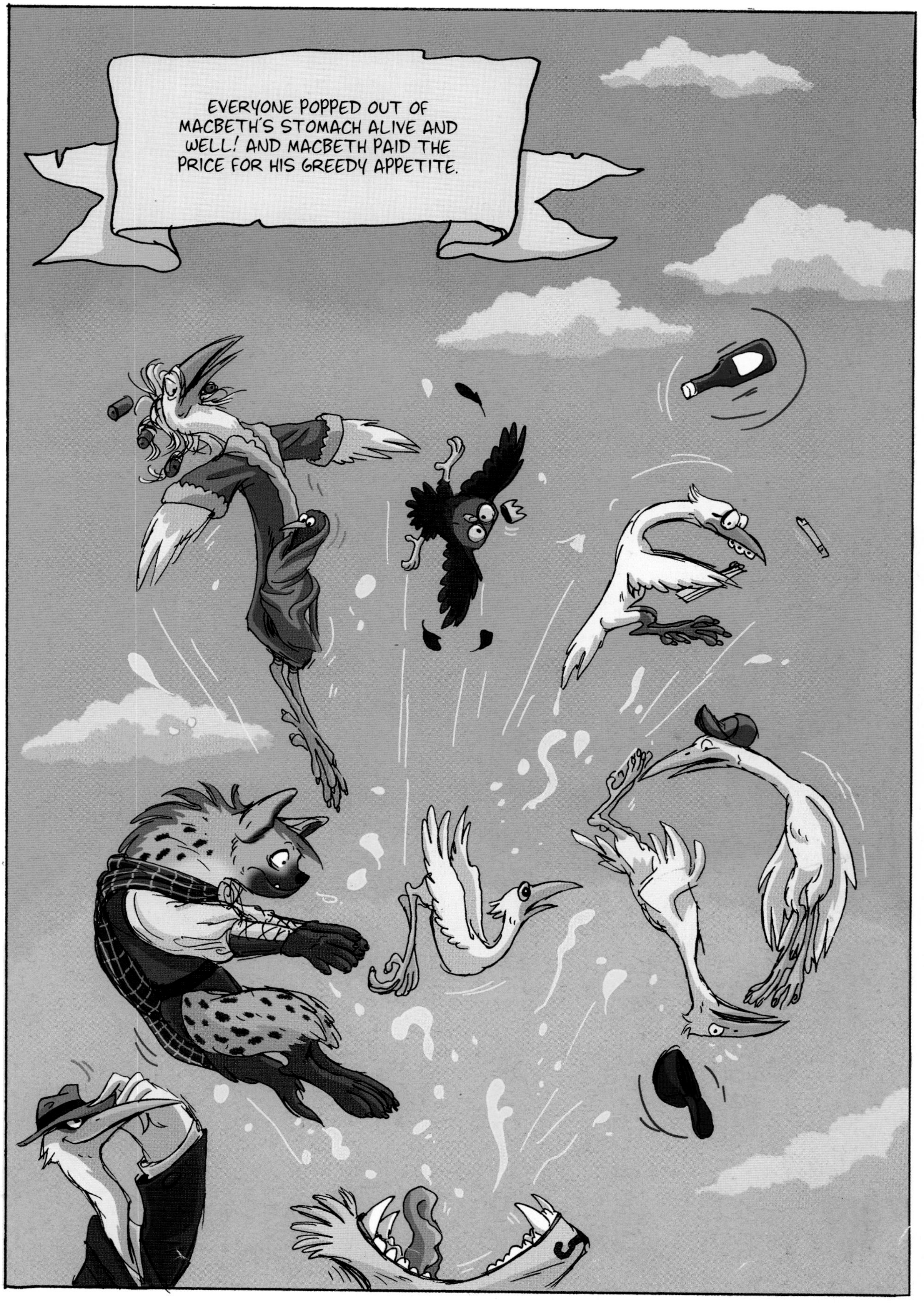
EVERYONE POPPED OUT OF MACBETH'S STOMACH ALIVE AND WELL! AND MACBETH PAID THE PRICE FOR HIS GREEDY APPETITE.

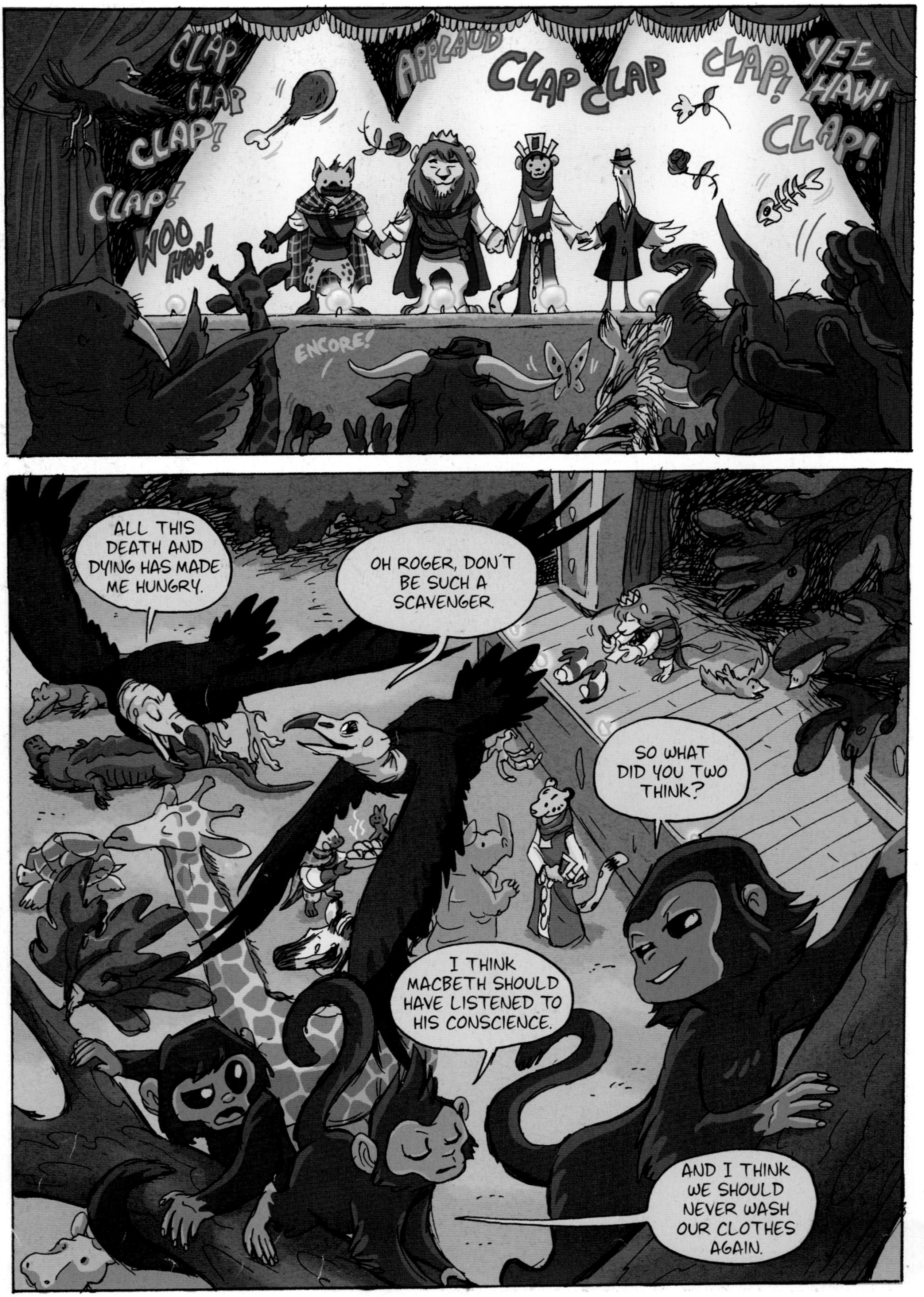
CLAP
CLAP
CLAP!
CLAP!
WOO HOO!
APPLAUD
CLAP CLAP
CLAP!
YEE HAW!
CLAP!
ENCORE!
ALL THIS DEATH AND DYING HAS MADE ME HUNGRY.
OH ROGER, DON'T BE SUCH A SCAVENGER.
SO WHAT DID YOU TWO THINK?
I THINK MACBETH SHOULD HAVE LISTENED TO HIS CONSCIENCE.
AND I THINK WE SHOULD NEVER WASH OUR CLOTHES AGAIN.

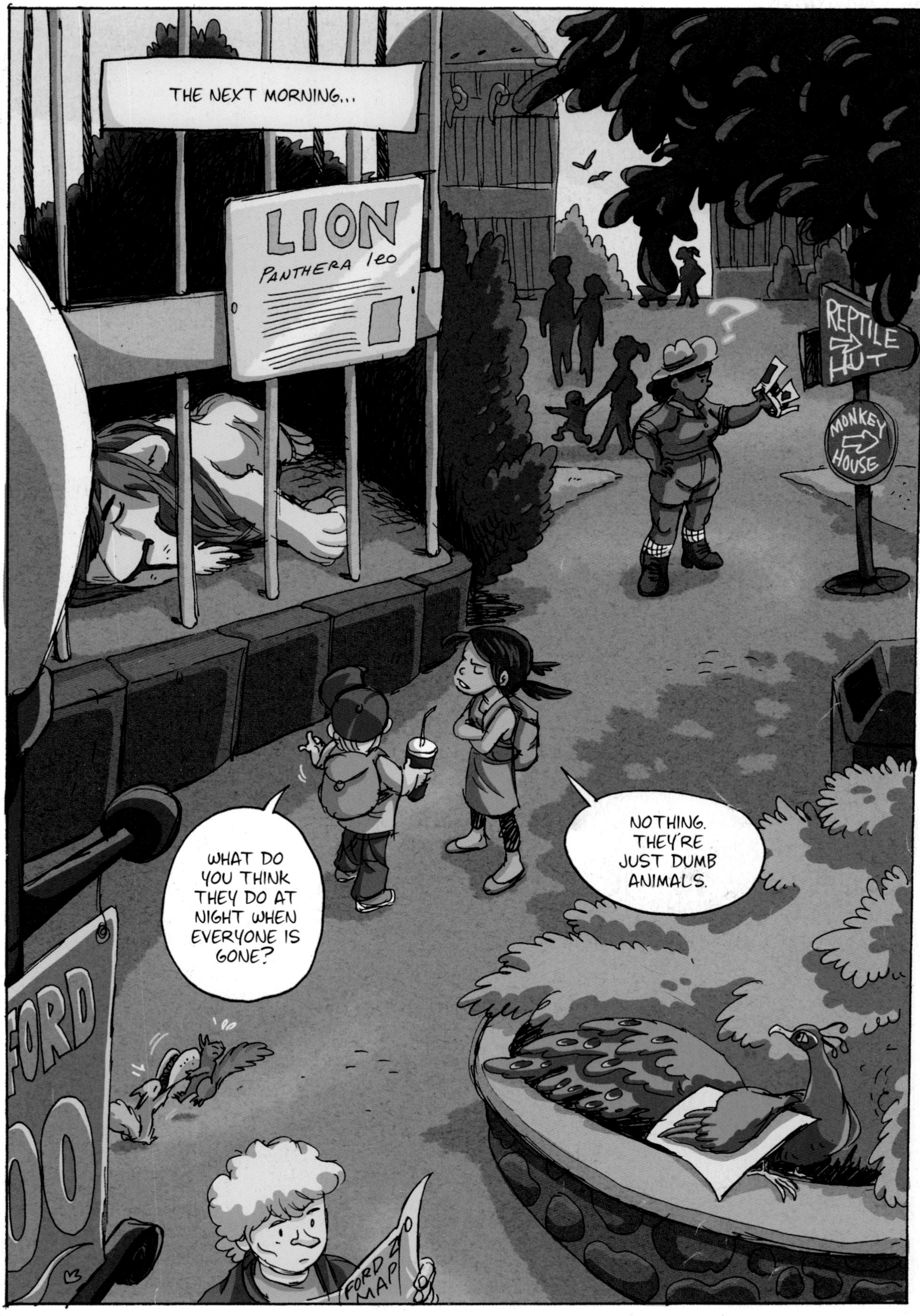
THE NEXT MORNING...
LION
PANTHERA leo
REPTILE HUT
MONKEY HOUSE
WHAT DO YOU THINK THEY DO AT NIGHT WHEN EVERYONE IS GONE?
NOTHING. THEY'RE JUST DUMB ANIMALS.
FORD ZOO
FORD ZOO MAP

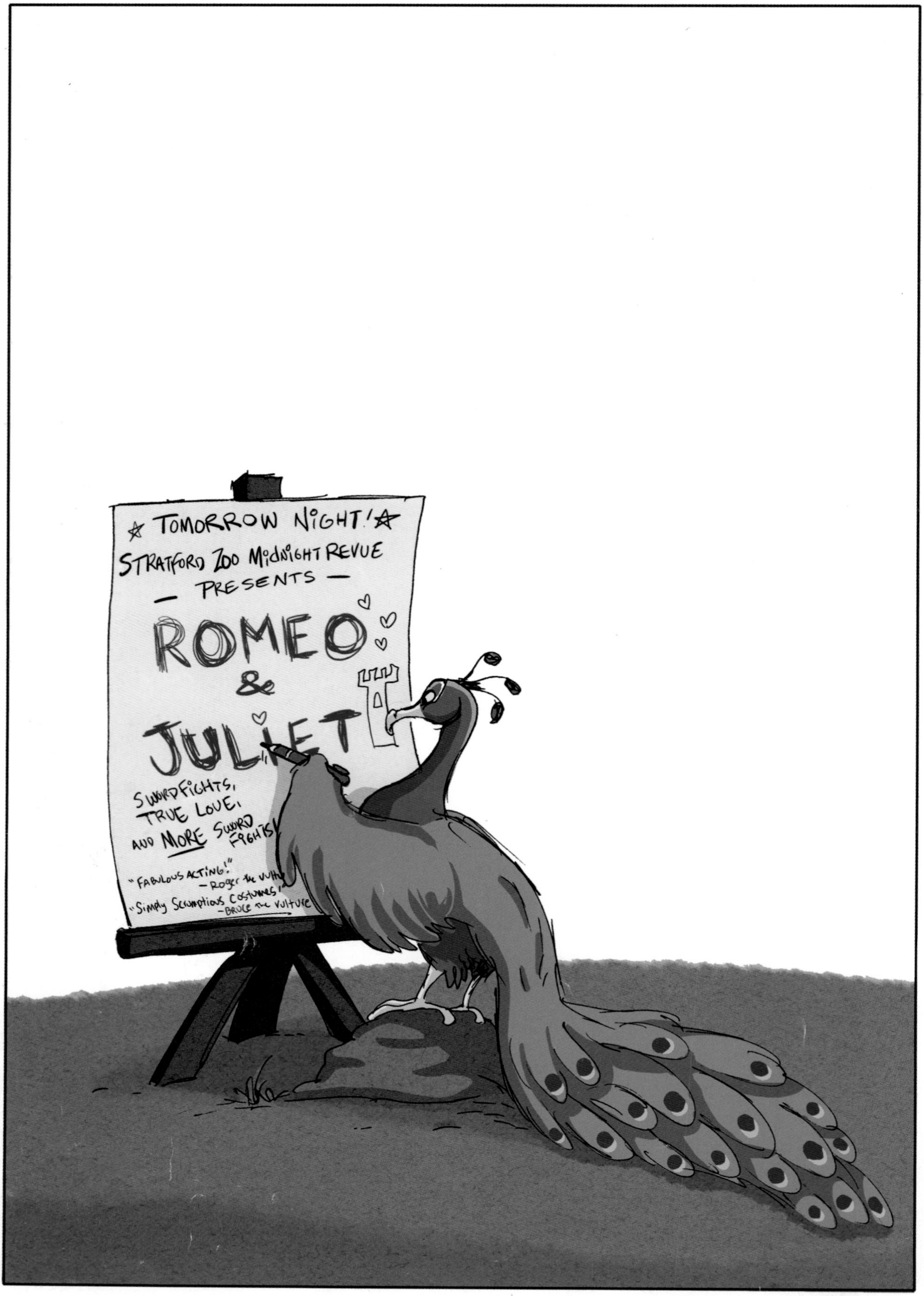
★ TOMORROW NIGHT! ★
STRATFORD ZOO MIDNIGHT REVUE
— PRESENTS —
ROMEO
&
JULIET
SWORDFIGHTS,
TRUE LOVE,
AND MORE SWORD FIGHTS!
"FABULOUS ACTING!"
—Roger the vult
"Simply Scrumptious Costumes!"
—BRUCE the vulture